HAMLET'S QUEST

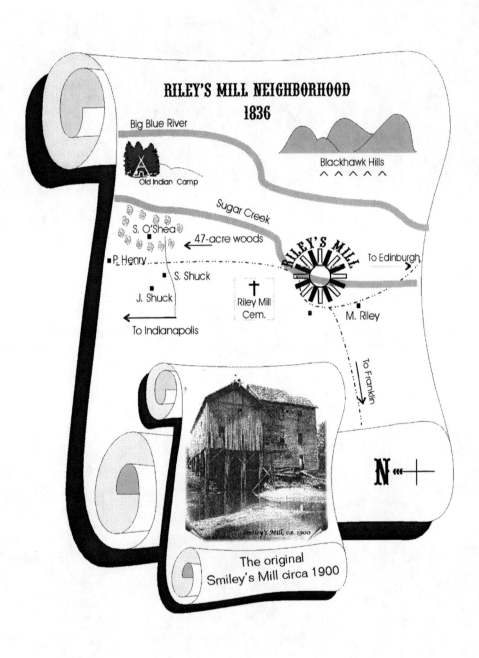

RILEY'S MILL NEIGHBORHOOD
1836

Big Blue River

Blackhawk Hills

Old Indian Camp

Sugar Creek

S. O'Shea

47-acre woods

P. Henry

S. Shuck

J. Shuck

Riley Mill Cem.

RILEY'S MILL

To Edinburgh

M. Riley

To Indianapolis

To Franklin

Smiley's Mill, ca. 1900

The original
Smiley's Mill circa 1900

N

HAMLET'S QUEST

"The Sugar Creek Anthologies of Jesse Freedom" Series Book Two

Young Adult

Judith Fowler Robbins

iUniverse, Inc.

New York Lincoln Shanghai

Hamlet's Quest
"The Sugar Creek Anthologies of Jesse Freedom"
Series Book Two

iUniverse, Inc.

For information address:
iUniverse, Inc.
2021 Pine Lake Road, Suite 100
Lincoln, NE 68512
www.iuniverse.com

Any resemblance to actual people and events is purely coincidental.
This is a work of fiction.

ISBN: 0-595-30084-7

Printed in the United States of America

Dedicated to the
Sugar Creek inhabitants:
Then and Now.

Woods door

By William Bridges

I'd slipped my mother's survey,
Most careless of sons;
I was too new to say
if I was anyone's.

The path, if path, by the husk
of a winter-killed row
led on into a dusk
of trees, I'd say now.

But trees had been few before,
and it seemed little odd
there should be the shape of a door
and coiled stones in the sod.

In the last yellow light
of a child's long day,
something held me that wasn't fright
before I was called away.

But it left me changed in the mind,
and ever since then
I've half expected to find
a door in a woods again.

CONTENTS

Part Four: The Next Generation

ILLUSTRATIONS

The author using CorelDraw and Corel Photopaint composed the illustrations in the book.

Fairies are the embodiment of
singular fates.

THE CAST

INDIANS

Black Hawk	Sauk war chief
Singing Bird	Wife of Black Hawk
Tecumseh	Shawnee war chief
White Cloud	Winnebago friend of Black Hawk
White Panther	Cherokee basket weaver

CHARACTERS

Parker Louis	North Georgia innkeeper
Aurora Louis	Wife of Parker Louis
Anna Louis	Daughter of Parker and Aurora Louis
Shane O'Shea	Pioneer Irish settler
Rose O'Shea	English wife of Shane O'Shea
Keren-happuck O'Shea	Daughter of Shane and Rose O'Shea
Sparrow O'Shea	Mother of Shane O'Shea
Gisela Puck	Widow on Feldberg
Wolf Puck	Grandson of Gisela Puck
John Riley	Pioneer sheriff and miller
Maggie Riley	Wife of John Riley
Mack Riley	Son of John and Maggie Riley, a physician
Elizabeth "Lizzy" Riley	Daughter of Mack Riley and Keren O'Shea
Johann von Shuck	German artist
Gertrude Shuck	Wife of Johann Shuck
Claire Shuck (Sparrow)	Daughter of Johann and Gertrude Shuck
Clovis Shuck (Hamlet)	Son of Johann and Gertrude Shuck

Samuel Shuck	Son of Hamlet and Anna Shuck
Abigail Shuck	Wife of Samuel Shuck
Jon Shuck	Son of Hamlet and Abigail Shuck
Jesse Shuck	Wife of Jon Shuck
John Clay Shuck	Son of Jon and Jesse Shuck

SPIRITS

Oberon	King of Fairies
Titania	Queen of Fairies
Pitt	English Brownie fairy
Keen	Irish Banshee fairy
Katrina	German Female Nix fairy
Friedrich	German Male Nix fairy
Watcher	Enchanted owl
Chelsea	Enchanted ground squirrel
Black Hawk	Enchanted hawk

INTRODUCTION

An old Indiana gristmill stood at the intersection of the Smiley Mill Road and the Greensburg Road in Johnson County for 83 years. Built in 1822, John Smiley, one of those hearty Midwestern renaissance men, built Smiley's Mill (Riley's Mill in the story). Gone now, with hardly a trace, its mill wheel still turns in the minds of those who watch the water run over the ruins of its dam across Sugar Creek. The following article from the Johnson County Museum gives a history of the mill, which is important as an Indiana landmark.

Article Source: **Nostalgia News**, *The Johnson County Historical Museum, Franklin, Indiana, October 1, 1978, Issue No. 6, p. 12.*

Major John Smiley, born in Nelson County, Ky. in 1781, came north through Washington County, In., in search of a mill site. He settled for a place on Sugar Creek in Needham Twp. which is now 5 miles south east of Franklin on the Greensburg Road, at the intersection of 700 E. Here he built a saw and gristmill, and just northeast of the mill, Smiley built his cabin. At this cabin, following the March 8, 1823, elections, the organization of the county took place. Judge William Watson Wick held the first court in the Smiley cabin, on October 16, 1823. John Smiley was the first sheriff of Johnson County.

The present channel for Sugar Creek, just south of Camp Comfort to the Smiley's Mill Bridge is the millrace. The bayou, or old bed of the creek, is on the east side of the bridge, looking north. The Smiley dam was made of logs. The WPA (Works Progress Administration) built the present dam in the 1930's by the W P A (Works Progress Administration), under the supervision of Barnett Fox, was built of enormous beams and huge boulders.

The Smiley's Mill brick school was located just north of the cemetery and east of John Smiley's cabin in a grove of walnut trees. John
Smiley died in 1854 and is buried in the Smiley cemetery.

The mill continued to be operated by members of the Smiley
family until after the turn of the century. William Smiley's Amity
MM copper stencil, used for marking bags of flour and meal, was
given to the museum by Mrs. Louis 0. Johnson, and may be seen in
the farm room. Dr. Robert Hougham recalled having his hair cut at
the mill as a child.

Vincent Shipp lived just north of the mill and taught music—he
also organized a small orchestra from his pupils.

The sawmill was removed from the grist mill near 1900, and the
timbers holding the gristmill rapidly deteriorated, causing the
remaining building to fall into the creek in 1905...

The mill stood in the western shadows of the low, rolling Black Hawk Hills
of neighboring Shelby County. Time has not changed the terrain around the
mill community very much save that, the forest is a fraction of the size it was in
the early 19th Century. Historical markers, tombstones in Smiley Mill
Cemetery, and Sugar Creek alone remain where all the first local settlers made
their homes and formed a community of souls who worked together to tame
the land. Over the past 181 years, many stories have risen about the lives of
those who lived on the land, generation after generation, season after season.

Before 1822, the Original Native Americans lived their own stories in the
same place. The land was theirs to tend, the land was the pioneers' to tend, the
land is ours to tend, and the land will be that of future generations to look
after. It is a nurturing place on Mother Earth, which only a few fortunate
people know.

It is not feasible to try to separate the footprints of the retreating Indiana
natives from those of the incoming pioneers at the cusp of the 19th Century. A
new nation of Sugar Creek settlers stepped into the moccasin prints of the
ancestral Sugar Creek peoples before the dust settled on the Trail of Tears.

Written in contemporary England by Richard Davey, these melancholy
lines could just as describe the American Indians:

> *This was thy home, then, gentle Jane!*
> *This thy green solitude; and here*
> *At evening, from thy gleaming pane,*
> *Thine eyes oft watched the dappled deer*

(Whilst the soft sun was in its wane)
Browsing beside the brooklet clear.
The brook yet runs, the sun sets now,
The deer still browseth—where art thou?

The "Jane" written about in the lines above was Lady Jane Gray, the beheaded nine-day queen of England. Immigrants to America had sought a less tyrannical society in which to live. Alas, in the doing, those trying to escape the executioner allegorically beheaded the "gentle Indian" who had lived in his own "green solitude" on this continent. The element of evil will never be more than another beheaded un-civilization away; yet, in the midst of it, there will be times of well being. When one sits beside a gentle creek under the same soft, warm sun that was Lady Jane's, the quest for civilization is re-crowned and, for a while, the steadfast deer browse peacefully everywhere.

SPECIAL THANKS

To the Smiley Mill 4-H Club
Members and Leaders
1982-1984
Who helped research The Sugar Creek Anthologies.

1982 Club Members:
Sean Crabbs, Chris Cummings, Amy Hensley, Amy Jackson, Jeff Jackson, Brian Klem, Jenny Liggett, Jill Liggett, Andy Lynch, Joe Lynch, Tony Lynch, Jenny Marchant, Jennifer Nicley, Deanna Pridemore, Jennifer Pridemore, Wayne Reynolds, Brian Shepard, Jimmy Taulman, Cara Vornehm,
Mini Club Members:
Dawn Crabbs, Dusty Fulkerson, Mark Hensley, Rita Reynolds
1984 Club Members:
Kirk Bartlett, Marla Burton, Brent Colburn, Brian Colburn, Dawn Crabbs, Sean Crabbs, Chris Cummings, Billy Demaree, Deanna Demaree, Delaine Eads, Shannon Eads, Shane Fleener, Dusty Fulkerson, Amy Hensley, Andy Hensley, Mark Hensley, Jennifer Hine, Amy Jackson, Jeff Jackson, Melissa Kaiser, Brian Klem, Jennifer Liggett, Jill Liggett, Jennifer Marchant, Wendy Mitchell, Jennifer Nicley, Rita Reynolds, Wayne Reynolds, Brian Shepard, Tom Shepherd, Tracy Shepherd, Anna Smithey, Jennifer Spence, Jimmy Stevens, James Taulman, Michelle Vest
Leaders:
Linda Hensley, Pat Jackson, Judy Liggett

Additional thanks to:

Rachael Henry, for her Smiley Mill research and her willingness to share
William Bridges, for his encouragement and assistance
Michael Robbins, for his constant support and love

PART ONE

THE LEGEND OF
WHITE PANTHER

CHAPTER I

HAMLET'S WORLD

Before I can tell you the story of Hamlet's quest, you need to hear about the long-ago world into which he was born and the various historical and personal accounts that set the stage for his life.

THE SHUCK FAMILY

Hamlet Shuck was a homeless boy who lived in a pre-electronic age when the storyteller had an honored place. His own story is told in the rhythm of a time when fairies were real, and life moved deliberately. Modern thrill-seekers might be shocked to learn the truth about the origins of their favorite nether-world elf queens and evil sorcerers.

Of German descent, Hamlet's one fervent wish is to unravel the tangled threads of his ancestry. To that end, he travels many unlikely roads to find his roots. He spent his childhood at a Spanish mission in St. Augustine, where he became a master weaver at a very young age. After a seven-year apprenticeship in the sweltering hacienda-style workshops of the Mission Nombre de Dios, Hamlet set out on a quest to find his parents. His journey took him to the misty haunts of the North Georgia Mountains, where superstition, legend and storytelling are a part of everyday life.

While traveling through the wilderness, he made friends with a young Indian named White Panther, who shared with him a Cherokee legend, which was to set Hamlet's path. Eventually, the weaver, who by then was a widower with a two-year old son named Samuel, settled in Indiana to homestead in the

Riley's Mill community. Samuel took over the farm while he was still in his teens, and Hamlet moved to Indianapolis, a growing frontier city, to set up a weaving studio in an artist colony there. The Shuck generations evolved: Samuel soon married and had a son of his own, whom he and Abigail called Jon; Jon married his sweetheart, Jesse, and their son was John Clay. Moreover, in the mix of it all, Hamlet discovered that he had a long-lost twin sister: Sparrow O'Shea.

The O'Shea Family

The Irish widow, Sparrow, came to the mill community rather late in Hamlet's life. He had been gone from the homestead for many years when Shane O'Shea, a neighbor down the creek from the Shuck farm, brought his mother to America from Ireland after his father died. Now, when Shane and his wife, Rose, first came to Sugar Creek, they moved into an abandoned log cabin. Rose was expecting their first child, Keren-happuck, and the rigors of their journey into Indiana had forced them to settle just where they were.

Keren-happuck and Jon Shuck grew up as contemporaries, though they did not know each other well as children. The protocol of that early day dictated that children stay busy as productive family members. As well, Rose and Shane were a bit overprotective of their stunning redheaded daughter and kept her close to home. On the other hand, Jon and the few other boys in the neighborhood often accompanied their fathers to the mill, the heartbeat of the community. As boys, Jon and the miller's son, Mack Riley, became close friends.

Little did anyone know about the kinship between Hamlet and Sparrow until, quite by accident, their grandchildren, Jon and Keren-happuck, made the fascinating discovery that they had matching silver pendants, gifts from their grandparents.

The Riley Family

John Riley came to Indiana in 1822 in search of a place to build a mill. His gristmill became the hub of activity where the neighbors on Sugar Creek met and exchanged stories. John became the first sheriff of the county. He and his wife, Maggie, had two sons, Mack and Sam. Hamlet had never known much about Sam; but he knew that the boy, Mack, was a doctor and had married Keren-happuck O'Shea.

Another person, who will profoundly influence Hamlet on his quest, is a Native American called Black Hawk, a Sauk war leader. As the story unfolds, the Indian becomes the nemesis of Hamlet's sister: Sparrow. Black Hawk's involvement with Sparrow came late in the warrior's life...Oh, dear! I'm getting the cart before the horse.

To begin to understand the land through which Hamlet traveled on his identity quest, one really should start by hearing the legend which Hamlet's Cherokee friend, White Panther, told him. Listen.

"... a snow-white panther appeared at the edge of an Appalachian woods primeval upon the Eastern Delta of the American continent."

Chapter 2

The Legend of White Panther

The Delta and the Young Panther

Once upon a time, when time was new...

A snow-white panther appeared at the edge of an Appalachian wood primeval upon the Eastern Delta of the American continent. He was young, only seven feet long, nose to tip of tail. Motionless, the animal squint his eyes and scanned the distance between him and an emerald lagoon. Ears poised, he listened for any sound of an intruder into his evening retreat. Only the calls of night birds and the heavy perfume from hanging wisteria drifted upon the breeze. "I love this peaceful place where everything is good," he whispered to himself.

The panther stretched, yawned, and then walked down to the water. Thirsty and hungry after sleeping all day in his cave, he drank deeply. The late afternoon sun behind him caused his long shadow to fall across the mirror of water. The young cat looked bigger than he actually was because the soft ripples exaggerated his image. He boasted with a shrill cry. The cavalier cat sauntered a few feet away and then sprang to a boulder to survey the clearing and enjoy the vespers of twilight.

Darkness fell while the beast on the rock groomed himself before going out in the marshes and along the sand bars to hunt food for his family.

Momentarily, the panther heard a splash in the lagoon. He quickly looked up and saw a small water sprite jump out of the water. It pointed anxiously toward a path in the woods and then disappeared back into the ring of ripples.

The beast was uneasy because he knew the nixie was a messenger of misery. There was no other sound after that, but the animal knew…the animals always know when change is in the wind.

Then, he saw an azure haze crawling through the path and settling over everything. He became one with the lagoon, the wisteria and the rock upon which he laid—one with nature. White Panther looked into the mist and began to see dark moving masses forming in the distance. Entranced, he fixed his eyes while the images came closer and then settled in the theatre over the lagoon. He froze, like the great bolder overlooking the retreat, and watched as terrifying scenes unfolded before him.

In the nebula, he saw tumbling hillside brooks and waterfalls turn into rivers of sliding sand and silt. Next, he saw lagoons and streams filling up with solid sediment. In a third scene, he saw the earth shake and animals fleeing into the heavily wooded frontier. Last, he saw himself taking his young family away from their home in the cave. Then, in a prophetic moment, he saw himself as Premier Panther, leading the entire nation of panther prides away from the disaster in the delta. He would tuck away in his heart this call to lead—tell no one. Yawning, he dropped to his belly, rolled over, and went to sleep.

The moon was full and high when a white owl flew over the lagoon, his screech piercing the night. The panther jolted awake. He felt weak at first, as though he could hardly stand; but he quickly gained strength, which was born of inspiration from his vision. He felt the renaissance within him that would come to all of nature on the Cumberland Plateau.

Abandoning his plans for hunting that night, the young cat returned to his cave. Gathering his cubs and mate around him, he spoke with uncommon resolve about change.

"Tonight," he began, "we shall not eat the feast of the hunt. We shall, instead, fast and think upon our life in the Delta. Listen carefully, for I have something to say."

The cubs revered their father and eagerly settled down to hear him. He was, after all, White Panther, one of the wise young males from whom the new Premier Panther would one day be chosen and celebrated by all the creatures in the Appalachian Delta. They knew that, as usual, what they were about to be told would next be shared with all the cats in the pride, their father vying to demonstrate his wisdom to the others.

White Panther spoke. "Long before this place was our home, the land was different. Whether water or fire covered it, I do not know. It does not matter. The thing that does matter is that even though the land changed, whatever happened here happened for good. Do you know why, little ones? It is because this is a perfect place for panthers to live. Not only do we have plenty of food and water, but also the beauty in the Delta is special; nothing is more beautiful than one's home. This realm was here long before we came and it will be here long after we are gone.

"Only a small part of life is about living and dying. The true essence of life, I promise you, is change. This land will soon change again and the panthers will have to find new homes. As we go, we will not fear change. Rather, if we must fear anything, it will be that there will be no change. For when life stops changing, the whole of nature will perish."

Ages passed, White Panther's vision came to pass.

A mysterious force from the southeast caused the African and North American continents to collide on the ocean floor. All in the slow motion of geologic time, new rock emerged from the depths to push aside old rock. Great slabs, miles across, pushed upward, tilted, and folded on top of themselves. The eruption crept up onto the North American continent, causing the earth below the delta for hundreds of miles to heave and rumble.

The rivers and streams flowing from the highlands of the Delta dumped tons of sediment into the lagoons and meandering channels below them, and the animals fled into the frontier where wild flowers flourished. Where there was once a balance of forest and water, grass and lagoon, only a plateau of sandstone and floodplain remained, ridges forming across its eastern boundary.

From the young panther of the delta, Hamlet learned to accept the casualties that alter a young man's life. An orphan, he survived his childhood years, intact.

THE PLATEAU AND THE RENAISSANCE PANTHER

Millennia later, A snow-white panther appeared at the edge of a sweet-smelling, wild-flowered frontier forest that bordered the ridged and sediment-filled plateau. Premier Panther of the Eastern Woodlands, he was eight feet long, nose to tip of tail. Having emerged from the depths of his cave in the heavily wooded interior, he was purring contentedly as he thought of his mate and their young cubs. The next moment he became silent and shuddered, for his eyes were on the desolate plateau. "This place was once peaceful and good—a paradise of lagoons and hanging vines of purple blooms. "But now," he hissed, "it is barren from here to the ever-growing ridges."

Ears poised, he listened for any sound of an intruder into his evening quest. He was planning a retreat to the ancient home cave of the Family of Premier

Cats. Through centuries of instinct, honed from the inherited memories of past generations, he knew of the cave where the first premier panther had reigned. That first great cat's color, a coat as pure as the arctic snow, stood for truth and purity. It had been a sign to the ancients that the spirits favored the regal white bloodline above all others to lead the Eastern Prides.

Thus, the Renaissance Panther, now recognized as the Premier White Panther, had led the animals through the dawn of a new age and into a new era. On their journey through time, the panthers had crossed the barren old lands and their prides had dwindled in number. At last, they were once again thriving in the lush green inland forest. Was his mission finished? Was he to continue to guide the prides? If so, he needed renewal for he now felt few challenges to motivate him. As leader, he felt a strong call to go on retreat to the cave of his fathers.

Motionless, White Panther narrowed his eyes and scanned the shadowy distance between him and an escarpment of high, white ridges. He wondered whether his fatherland cave could have escaped ruin during the disaster in the delta. He was on a mission to find out. His trip across the sun-baked plateau would take two nights. He would have to spend one day with no water in the open wasteland. He thought he would stop at the site of the ancient lagoon where so many years ago the Premier Panther had received the vision of changes to come.

He began to walk. He walked all night and, in the morning, indeed came to the spot where sweet-smelling wisteria once floated on the evening breeze. Was that hinting of the scent only his imagination? He hoped that the memory of the cool, clear lagoon buried in the depths of time would sustain him through the day. He lay down under the overhang of a low rock ridge to sleep over those memories and whispered, "Wouldn't it be wonderful if someday this soil was fertile again." The long morning shadows from the wall of white ridges behind him had stretched across the wasteland and died in the sun.

Something moved in the scrub grass beside him. Startled, he was up in an instant. His sun-blinded eyes saw the silhouette of a creature on two feet running away from him. "Could it have been a chipmunk?" he thought. "They often burrow out on the open plateau?" Soon, the intruder was out of sight and all was still. Uneasy, White Panther followed the trail in the brittle undergrowth left by his morning visitor. A strange scent that the panther did not recognize permeated the air along the way.

"This is a bad sign," the wise animal growled.

"Yes," a spirit said, "a bad omen."

In the path before him, White Panther saw the same nix his ancestor had seen at the lagoon before the woods cloud came. Now, the fairy looked like a shimmering shrew, draped with leaves from a lace flower. It glistened like dew on a spider's web when the sun's rays fell full upon it. Fear gripped him, for he knew this tiny being held strong powers.

"What comes?" demanded White Panther, rather more bravely than he felt.

"Man," answered the fairy. At the same time, she thrust a tiny dart into a bow she was carrying and shot it into the cat's paw.

"Ouch!" White Panther winced. "What is Man?" He dropped to the ground to dream.

The Ancient Cave of the first Premier Panther loomed before him, whole and untouched by the ravages of the ages. In the darkness inside the mouth of the cave, he saw the wispy face of his great ancestor, who was speaking to him. "All is well, my loyal descendant. This great cave is still intact; my spirit still lives, along with the spirits of all your famous elders.

"But, I must tell you that the time is not right for you to join us. There is still work for you to do on the old plateau. You must prepare the prides for yet another new age—an age in which the ridges will evolve into new tree-filled mountains and the plateau will become lush with rambling rivers and life-giving plants. All the animals may return if they wish to enjoy the riches of nature, which Providence will restore to the land.

"Now, listen to me. Leading the panthers in the era of promised new growth sounds like a simple task compared to what you have had to endure in the past. It would be, except for one thing. The Maker of the Universe has seen fit to introduce a new creature into your environment—Man. Along with the Age of New Mountains comes the Age of Man. Man comes as a new being, somewhat more like animals than plants and minerals, but his essence will be as mysterious as a fairy's. Man will be a riddle. He will be enemy; he will be friend. He will try to destroy you; he will try to save you."

The ancient panther was starting to fade. "Although you will have to contend with the mystery of Man, you will be allowed to return to this Cave of the Ancients when the New Mountain building is accomplished. Do what is required; your own great adventure waits here in the land of your beginnings. This is my solemn promise."

Just before dusk, a gentle rain began to fall upon the panther in the path, quietly awakening him. He felt the sting of a splinter in his paw and worked it out with his teeth. White Panther did not resume his quest for spiritual guidance, for he had had a vision. He returned instead to his den in the forest.

Gathering his cubs and mate around him, he spoke about his dream of the ancient home of the panthers. His family listened carefully because he was the celebrated Premier Panther, who led all the prides from the western frontier to the ocean in the east. They knew that, again, they would be first to hear prophesy about change, which was revealed only to white panthers of premier lineage. Then, tomorrow, all the prides would hear the news.

White Panther began. The message was not a new one:

"Long before the frontier was our home, the sediment fields out there formed into one beautiful delta, which was covered with lagoons and hanging purple wisteria. Since you were not there, you cannot know. It does not matter. The thing that does matter is that even though the land has changed, whatever happened here happened for good. Do you know why, little ones? It is because this forested land is perfect for us. Not only do we have plenty of food and water, but also the beauty on the frontier is special because this is our home—nothing is more beautiful than one's home. This realm was here long before we came and it will be here long after we are gone.

"Only a small part of life is about living and dying. However, the true essence of life, I promise you, is change. The ridges will become New Mountains; the barren sediment fields will become lush. We panthers will be able to repopulate our homeland or to stay here. As we go, we will not fear change. Rather, if we must fear anything, it will be that there will be no change. For when life stops changing, the whole of nature will perish."

Time passed...

The land, once delta, then sediment fields and low ridges, changed into the Great Appalachian Mountains and the flourishing Cumberland Plateau, where rivers ran and life abounded. The panthers and all the other beasts, having fled the land during the barren times, were anxious to return to the new valleys, the rambling rivers, and the mountain ranges, with their stone arches and hearty waterfalls. By then, they knew about Man and lived mostly in peace alongside him.

From the Renaissance Panther, Hamlet learned that time cannot destroy a man's roots. As time passed, he grew in stature and in the knowledge that each generation builds upon the discoveries of its forebears.

THE MOUNTAINS & THE OLD PANTHER

50,000 BC. The Cherokee legend, told around both Indian and settler campfires in the cold mountain villages, had been paramount in Hamlet's education into life's ways.

An old, snow-white panther crept out of his cave and appeared at the edge of dense woods. He was nine-foot long, nose to tip of tail. Motionless, he narrowed his eyes and scanned the distance between him and the wall of high, white mountains that were once only ridges upon sediment fields.

Ears poised, he listened for any sound of an intruder into his evening venture: by now, early Man sometimes crossed his path. He was planning a journey through the Plateau to be sure his prides had made good homes, as he had on the sacred spot over the purple lagoon. When he first discovered the crystal water flowing from the ground there, he knew it was a sign to bring his family. He believed that the spring was born from his lagoon of old.

He lay down to watch the long shadows of evening stretch across the Plateau, fingering the southern reaches of the New Mountains. He noticed a bright falling star, and then fell off to slumber. The tiny star had left its celestial orbit and was speeding to Earth on the wings of his age-old fairy of prophecies, the nix.

A vision came before him. Once again, it was the cave of his ancestors. He saw the Ancient Premier Panther and heard his voice. "Your homeland has been restored to a wonderful Plateau and the ridges have turned into majestic New Mountains.

"If you choose, you may live for a while longer in your den over the old lagoon," the Ancient continued. "But once, I promised that after the New Mountain Age you could come to the Cave of the Ancients, where a great adventure awaits you. It is according to that pledge that I will now reveal something of the future.

"Soon, the panther prides will no longer be safe on the Plateau. It is ordained, for a while at least, for Man rule and for much wildlife to perish. When you come to the ancient cave, your mission will be twofold: first, to preserve its great secret—that it is our tunnel back to Creation and our doorway out to Creator. Until now, only the original natives realize that it is sacred ground. Secondly, you are to ensure safe passage into the new frontier for men of adventure, women of courage and children of change. The destiny of many a man will depend on you. Humankind will name this place the Cumberland Gap and the formidable mountains through which it passes, the Appalachians.

"You may join the Ancients now, when you choose."

When he awoke from his dream, the fairy nix was sitting on the small shooting star, which had come to rest near White Panther. "The time has come," she said. "Prepare your prides for choosing a new leader." In a blink of the cat's eye, the star extinguished and the nix disappeared.

White Panther arose and gave a great summoning scream to all the prides. When the panthers heard it, they knew that their old leader was leaving them. They had sensed for some time that a new leader would soon rise among them, because White Panther often talked about returning to the Ancient Cave. Panthers never die, they return to the Ancients.

All knew that when he left, the prides would have their councils and contests to choose a new leader. First, however, they would all gather one last time at the Premier Panther's cave—a spot where, once in the long ago, a wisteria-scented lagoon rippled. When they had all gathered, they would receive parting words of wisdom from the old leader.

"A change is coming," White Panther began. "I shall be leaving you, now. I am going on a great adventure, a mission about which I am not at liberty to tell you. Just know that you must choose a new leader. The spirit of the Ancient Panthers will guide you in making your choice. Watch and listen for their counsel."

The panthers were quiet. They would miss the kindly old Premier. They couldn't remember when he was not there.

"In this life, if I have learned anything, it is to be content wherever I am. Home is the most beautiful place in the world. It is the key to well being. I have glimpsed by new life. I humbly tell you that I shall reside in the sacred Ancient Cave of the Premiers. The spirit of the Most Ancient of Ancients has visited me three times. Upon the last, it gave me leave to come and live forever in the best, most beautiful cave of all.

"Remember, changes will come to you, too. Welcome them, because if life stops changing, the whole of nature will perish. Make your new homes, find beauty in them and be content. Someday, when the time comes for you to return to the ancients, you may go without fear; because it will be your best home of all."

Silence permeated the woods. White Panther arose, tucked one front leg under him, and gave a low bow. When he stood up, he said, "I am going now; tomorrow I will wake up in the cave of our ancestors. There I shall find a new life, a life for which I have waited a long, long time."

Quietly, he turned and walked gracefully into the woods.

Time passed and humankind came...

White Panther reached the cave of his ancestors. The great, snowy beast still roams the land of his ancients—a place now called the Land of the Cherokee and the Great Cumberland Gap.

From the old panther, Hamlet learned that good things wait for those who persevere. For the length of his life, the weaver's tenacious and steady pace allowed him to stay on the path to discovery.

PART TWO

SPARROW AND THE SAUK WAR CHIEF

CHAPTER 3

MYSTERIOUS SPARROW

Just as sure as the mountains in the Eastern Woodlands had risen from the depths of the Atlantic, change had come to the lives of the Sugar Creek settlers. Now comes the next generation of the Families O'Shea, Riley and Shuck. They are waiting for you, just where we left them at the end of American Spirits, Book One.

The night is black between frequent daggers of lightning that pierce the O'Shea's 47-acre woods. Gathered in Shane and Rose's cabin are the old weaver, Hamlet Shuck; his son, Samuel, whose wife Abigail was at home with John Clay, their grandchild; and his grandson and wife, Jon and Jesse. With them are the O'Sheas' daughter, Keren-happuck; her new husband, Dr. Mack Riley; and Shane's mother, Sparrow O'Shea, an herbal healer. They had all just been shocked into silence, because two matching silver pieces, Sparrow's locket and Hamlet's watch fob, had magically opened before their eyes.

Sparrow O'Shea searched her brother's face. Whether Hamlet was a long-lost twin or not, she'd had enough. There were so many things the woman could have said, could have asked; but she uttered only one word, "Tomorrow." Throwing her shawl over her head and shoulders, the grandmother lifted her long skirt and apron and stepped over the hand-hewn maple threshold worn smooth from generations of footsteps. The tall, gently bent figure moved down the field-rock footpath, cane in hand, oblivious to the rain and lightning ghosts that charged the air around her. When she disappeared into the barn, Shane closed the cabin door and then turned to face the stunned old weaver. "That, Uncle, was your sister. Tomorrow, after a good night's sleep, maybe she'll be a little more congenial."

Hamlet didn't know what to say. He walked over to the window to look toward the barn. A flicker of candlelight came from a window high up in the loft. "That where she lives? In the barn?"

"It is," Shane said.

The look of amazement and disbelief on Hamlet's face struck Shane's new son-in-law, Mack, as funny. Laughing softly, he picked up the conversation. "Yes Sir! She lives up there with a spoiled old peacock. By some accounts, she's the best doctor in the family!"

A quick chuckle ran through the room and Keren-happuck gave her husband a short rebuff. "Now, Mack! You promised!" Sparrow had many devotees in the community who preferred her tonics to getting in a doctor.

The pretty redhead turned, then, to Hamlet: "My husband is a doctor just starting his practice, but a lot of people around here have come to rely on Grandmother when they're ill. She's very good with herbal medicines."

Hamlet smiled and nodded, still a bit baffled at the woman's abrupt departure. He closed the silver watch fob in his hand and handed it back to his grandson. Looking back out the window, again, he said, "A peacock?" and then shook his head with wonder.

Jon looked down at the watch fob for a moment, in thought, and said, "No Grandfather, you should keep this for now."

Hamlet absently took the silver piece and slipped it in his pocket. "Looks like the rain is letting up, Son," he said to Samuel. "We'd better be going." Glancing at Jon and Jesse, he asked, "You two ready?" Jon nodded.

"Like she said," Samuel acknowledged his father, motioning toward the barn and Sparrow, 'tomorrow.' There's nothing more to do tonight."

"Uncle!" Shane called. "Here are your dancers! You don't want to forget them!"

Hamlet carefully folded the small tapestry of dancing children with matching pendants and put it in his pocket. It was his favorite weaving.

The Shucks took their cloaks off the wall pegs, covered their heads, and scurried to their carriage. Rose called to them: "You all come on back tomorrow evening and bring Abigail. We'll have a real homecoming celebration for you Hamlet! If it's a nice day, we'll eat outside—have a picnic! About four o'clock?"

Visitors gone, Shane picked up his cherry wood fiddle, tucked it under his chin and slowly drew the bow across its strings. For a long moment, he stood quietly, lost in thought, waiting for the sound to fade. His eyes toyed with the winking-eye knot on the front of the fiddle. Without playing another note, he hung it back in its place on the wall.

In bed, Shane and Rose lay in the dark trying to sleep. "Shane," she said.

"Huh?"

"I could have sworn that eye on your father's fiddle winked when those pendants opened."

"I know. It could have been a dancing shadow from the candle. But, I have a feeling that Mother and Uncle Hamlet's father, the old violin maker himself, did make that fiddle and that he and his wife were here tonight with their long lost children."

Living together in an ancient sycamore in Shane's yard were three European sprites: a brownie, a banshee, and a nix, along with various American wood sprites. The "enchanted" had also been stunned by the revelation that Hamlet and Sparrow were twins.

Just now, out in the bewitched sycamore, Watcher, the ancient white owl who protected the domain of the 47-acre woods, was high on his perch. He was dreaming, perhaps, of his youth, of a time when his old joints did not complain of the damp. The brownie, Pitt, had gone to bed in his loft in the hollow of the tree where woodpeckers once lived. The nix, Katrina, who sometimes transformed into Mack's dog, lay just far enough inside the entrance of the tree to stay dry. She was keeping an eye out, between snoozes, for Mack and Keren to leave. When, at last, the newlyweds climbed into the carriage to go home, Kate made a mad dash across the lawn, leaped onto the seat, and rode home in her usual spot—between them.

The only fairy not accounted for in the tree was the banshee, Keen. However, that was not unusual. She often shared quarters with Grandmother Sparrow instead of sleeping in the enchanted tree. Earlier that evening, when the fairies left the cabin, Keen had gone straight to the barn to wait for the old banshee of a woman. The cup of chamomile tea she had brewed had worked its calming powers and left the fairy sound asleep, indeed.

Mysterious Sparrow on the path with
Brother Peacock

CHAPTER 4

A COLD NIGHT IN THE LOFT

The banshee, Keen, did not even stir when the grandmother came in out of the storm. Sparrow found the fairy sleeping in a basket of ear corn, little teacup still in hand, and shivering from the damp. She brought a small quilt, which she had made for Keen, and gently wrapped it around the banshee. On tiptoe, she carried her companion to her sleeping corner by the chimney.

Sparrow had made the banshee a charming little home in the trunk she had brought over on the ship when emigrating from Ireland. She covered it with a whimsical roof made from broom grass for an Irish-cottage look. Keen loved her cozy little home. Imagine! A banshee with a home of her own! She furnished it with a feather-stuffed sleeping tick and still had room for her own wee treasure chest. Of course, Keen really needed nothing—fairies are self-sustaining—but she liked the idea of having a feather bed and her own things. Her valuables included an eye from a peacock feather, a bag of dried lavender, a lock of Keren-happuck's hair, and a vial of her own genuine keening tears.

Sparrow lifted the roof and laid the sleeping banshee in her bed. Keen stirred only for a moment, and then nestled down in her tick to a deep sleep. Keen often fell asleep just any place around the loft and Sparrow was afraid of stepping on her. It was for that reason, mainly, that the grandmother had made the sea-chest cottage.

The woman was tired, bewildered at her brother's appearance, and very out of sorts. She sat in the dark in her wooden rocker and felt a chill from her wet clothes. "I wish it was winter so I could build a little fire to warm this place up," she mumbled. "On the other hand, why not build a fire? I'm shaking and I need to dry these clothes."

She got up from the chair, crossed the room to the door, and hurried down the hand-hewn stairs to the wood shop for kindling and a log to burn. She quickly gathered some scraps into her apron, but could see nothing big enough to sustain a fire. Then, she spied Shane's wood box next to the downstairs fireplace. Numb fingers lifted the lid. There was still enough firewood left to make a good fire.

"There," she said and then gathered up a piece. The air was damp and the wood was heavy. Toting her load, Sparrow grasped the handrail and dug her fingernails in for support as she climbed. By the time she reached the top of the steps, exhaustion had swept over her so completely that she could hardly breathe. Wearily, with stiff hands, she put the wood down on the hearth, arranged the kindling under it to suit her, and opened the damper. Taking a bit of hemp wool out of a pouch that hung from a peg on the mantle, she stuck it in the kindling and struck flint to spark a fire. A few puffs of breath on it and a blaze soon flamed.

Standing on the rug before the fire, she let her apron and dress slip to her ankles, and then sat in the rocker to remove her moccasins and the pins from her tangled hair. Realizing that even her under garments were wet, she took them off, too, and pulled a pieced quilt from the arm of the chair around her bare body.

Fleetingly, the grandmother thought of her younger years, when she had been a tall, well-built woman with auburn hair. Her body seemed a little smaller now, though her muscles were taut and her skin bore few of the wrinkles of most women her age. Her hair was like spun milkweed—the color of angel hair. She sighed.

Just now, Sparrow wished for something hot to warm her insides; but she was too miserable to move. The warmth from the fire felt good to her as she looked around the room in the dim light from the fireplace.

"We don't have time for this," she said irritably. "Why did he have to show up now? Maybe he is my brother, but I never knew him. I wonder how long he'll stay." She nervously rocked back and forth in her chair and closed her eyes.

"I have a much more pressing problem on my mind," she whispered. "There's no time for this twin foolishness now. I have to get back out in the woods to find out about that old Indian couple camping up in the Delaware ruins. The man was wearing the pouch of a medicine man. I think he is digging the bulbs of the wildflowers. Oh, well, I suppose that is okay but setting snares for an animal are out! That rascal has no business setting rabbit traps into which one of us, or the cows, could step. Ha! Bet he was surprised that I sprang his trap yesterday."

She poked the fire.

"On the other hand, I suppose they do have to eat. I barely caught a glimpse, but I know that was a woman I saw with him."

Sparrow's voice was getting louder with anger. "Indians! Why don't they settle down somewhere and farm for food like the rest of us? I just wonder what mischief they're up to!"

Keen, by now, was quite awake. "What on earth!" she muttered, getting herself up off the tick. "What's she on about now?" The banshee flitted to the hearth to see what ailed Sparrow. "What's wrong?"

Finding herself caught, Sparrow quickly changed the object of her immediate discontent with the Indians back to Hamlet. "That old man that was here today," she said, pointing toward the cabin. "What does he want, anyway?"

"Aren't you glad to find out that you have a brother, Miss Sparrow?"

"It's not that. I guess he is okay, but I have gone all my life without knowing him. Why start now? Now, of all times!"

"What do you mean, 'now of all times'?"

"Well," Sparrow said warily, "I guess that's my business. Does everybody have to know everything I do? I hate that! I hate it when people try to mind my business!" Sparrow suddenly realized that she might have said too much. The last thing she needed was a bunch of fairies to get in the way. If she were not careful, she would have them on her trail. They were always trying to look after her whether she needed it or not.

"Now, Miss Sparrow," the banshee reproached her, sensing that the scrappy old woman truly was up to something. "You know you can't hide things from me. At least, you never tried to before. What's going on?"

"Nothing," Sparrow said, getting up to fetch her sleeping gown from its peg beside the fireplace. "I'm going to fix a cup of chicory and go to bed. How about you? Would you like some chicory?"

"Are you changing the subject, Miss Sparrow?"

"Little Miss Busybody," Sparrow snapped. "Nothing that concerns you is going on. In fact, nothing is going on at all. Now, come along, let's heat some water."

Keen flew up to the cupboard for a chicory root. She knew something was up, but she also knew that Sparrow had spoken, so there was no use saying anything else. The two sipped from their steaming teacups in silence, and, soon the fairy was back in her little house snoozing away under her quilt.

When Keen woke up the next morning, the shadows of the leaves were dancing in the sunbeams like whirligigs on the floor. "Sunshine!" she thought. "The rain has stopped." Keen's happy face soon turned to a frown. Sparrow was gone. Her bed was cold, so the banshee knew she had been up for some time. "Oh, dear me. My mysterious old Sparrow, whatever are you doing? Where are you?"

The banshee first checked the chicken house, because that was usually Sparrow's first chore of the day—to open up the coop to feed and water the chickens. Sparrow was not there. Then, Keen checked the cabin: Rose and Shane were just getting up—no Sparrow. Next, she checked the landing on the creek bank where Sparrow sometimes fished for catfish in the early morning. No. Panic started to set in. Keen flew to the enchanted tree so fast that she was out of breath when she shot through the door.

"Pitt! Watcher! Wake up!" she cried, almost in hysterics.

Watcher jumped so high he lost his grip on the perch and fluttered to the floor. "My word, Keen. You nearly gave me a stroke! What on earth are you shouting about?"

"Sparrow is gone!" she gasped and jumped about with the speed of a hummingbird.

Pitt streaked down the grapevine from his woodpecker-hole sleeping chamber. "Sparrow? You know she has a propensity to stray."

Watcher could see that they were not going to find out much until they got Keen to settle down.

"There, there, my bouncing wee banshee," the old owl said in the most calming voice he could muster. "How can you ever expect us to understand you if you're all atwitter? Now, you just sit down here and tell us all about it."

Pitt rolled out a grass mat on which they sat. He remembered that sometimes the Irish widow seemed to lose herself in a sort of mournful chant. "Is Sparrow keening again?"

"No, no. She isn't keening," Keen said, settling down a bit. "I wish that's all it was. There's something else."

"Well, what? What is it?" Pitt was getting irritated.

"I don't know."

"What do you mean you don't know?" Pitt threw up his hands. "You said there was something else. What in the name of King Oberon is it?"

"I just don't know, I tell you!" Keen shook her head. "Last night she was very agitated—just sitting in front of the fire arguing with herself—loud! She was talking so loud she woke me up!"

"That doesn't sound so unusual for the grandmother," the owl hooted. "She's just naturally disputatious."

"No," the banshee shook her head. "It was different. I mean she was really in a state. Said something about why did Grandfather Hamlet have to show up now; talking about why did he had to turn up now of all times."

"Is that all?" Pitt asked. "That's nothing. She could have meant anything. You know she is as reclusive as a hermit crab. She just doesn't like anything to change around her."

"I'm sure you're right, Pitt," Watcher agreed.

"I tell you, this is not the same," Keen said. "There's more to it than being a loner. You have to remember, I have known her longer than I have known either of you. This banshee was with her back in Ireland from the time she was a toddler. But, maybe you're right; with Sparrow, I get too emotional."

"Why, Keen!" Pitt teased. "I never thought I'd hear you admit that!"

"Pitt!" Keen quipped, showing her irascible temper. "I'll show you emotional!" With that, she swatted at him, but he was too quick for her. He jumped back off the mat, howling with laughter, when she lost her balance and fell face first to the ground. "You fool!" she grumbled and huffed out of the tree. "I can see I'll get no help from you!"

Watcher flew after her and enfolded her in his gentle wings. "We'll look for her. We'll *all* look for her," he said looking back at Pitt in admonition.

The brownie tucked in his chin and sighed with resignation. "Okay. I have nothing else on tap for today anyway!"

The three were off into the early morning light in search of the grandmother.

Meanwhile, Sparrow was out in the deep woods, scanning the trail for signs of the Indian and his animal traps. She hardly felt the arrow graze her forehead before her world went black…

CHAPTER 5

YOUNG LIEUTENANT BLACK HAWK

The weaver Hamlet's sister, Sparrow, was not going to be easy to get to know, much less understand. He sensed, at first glance, that she was the epitome of eccentricity and that she earned each of the lines in her graphic face. He would be there for the next few days to witness just how Sparrow routinely added color to her life: this time she was absorbed in some Indians who had come through the neighborhood. In those days, it was nothing to see entire bands of hunter Indians running softly through the forest.

A gasp, a groan, Grandmother Sparrow fell into the pine needles on the damp forest floor. A dark stream of blood oozed from the arrow wound into a crease on her forehead and trickled across the bridge of her nose to puddle in one eye. Silver hair spread across her face, as if nature's caretakers were trying to hide the shame of the deed. She came to rest and did not move. Brother Peacock, as she liked to call her tamed bird, hissed wildly while his fan obtruded to its gorgeous metallic limits. For a panicky moment, time and motion crawled for the befuddled bird. Like a statue, he watched, horrified, unbelievingly from a distance not five feet from his fallen friend. Frozen, he cast his eyes about the scene and then into the depths of the darkening woods. Nothing moving. Still. Quiet, except for the red-eyed cicada choir. Slowly, gingerly the peacock lowered his eye-studded feathers into a train and his stiff, skinny legs took the few steps between him and Sparrow.

The puzzled bird looked down at the woman for a time and then nervously scratched the ground trying to rouse her. When he felt the wet, warm blood that was soaking into the earth from her head, he cooed and clucked not unlike a mother hen to try to raise his mistress. 'Twas to no avail. It was just the two of them, alone, in the woods. Then, for not being the brightest of birds, Brother Peacock did something rather heroic: he used the only means he had to help his Sparrow—the mystical eyes of his glorious plumes. He laid them down, one by one, to cover the wound to stop the bleeding and then nestled his warm body against her.

* * *

Now, to really understand the reason why Black Hawk was even setting traps in Shane O'Shea's woods, one has to go back many years to an experience he had as a young lieutenant in the Shawnee Tecumseh's fighting force.

So many times in the course of his life, the old Sauk war chief, Black Hawk, had said good-bye to Singing Bird—the beautiful black-haired love of his life. However, this time, her hair having turned silver with age, his wife was going with him. 'Twas not to some Indian war the two would journey but to a place through which a once-young Lieutenant Black Hawk had traveled with the famous Tecumseh. That was about 20 years before the Black Hawk War, during which, Black Hawk became a famous war chief. Sometimes, by chance, the trails that a man walks down lead him to fame, when all he is seeking is to find himself. It was like that with Black Hawk.

1812. BLACK HAWK DISCOVERS THE WOOD

During the War of 1812, Black Hawk had accompanied Tecumseh on a mission to recruit remnants of the Indiana Delaware tribe to join them in chasing the white settlers from Indian ancestral homelands. He had followed Tecumseh south into the great till plain in Indiana where the Lenni Lenape, their name for the Delaware Tribe, had once lived. Algonquin storytellers had often told a tale known everywhere of some "little people" and an old Delaware family who lived near a magic tree in the Indiana Territory.

Tecumseh's emissaries had followed the creeks—their road maps—to find the way to that sacred sycamore made so famous by Watcher, the last of the great Delaware chiefs to inhabit that land.

The day was gone when upon cats' paws the Indian party reached the high place between Shane O'Shea's house and that of Peter Henry, his closest neighbor. Could this be the site of the old Delaware town? Are remnants of the Lenape left? They wondered; thought not. Abandoned stone tools, once used by the now-vanished tribe, littered the ground beneath their moccasins. The hill on which they stood rose above the western bank of *Then-a-me-say*, the native word for Sugar Creek. Because of the many trees in this stretch of woodland, the traveling band did not see the small village of cabins and the huge gristmill that lay just out of sight beyond them. Nor did they hear the water wheel turning gracefully to drag fresh water up over its slats to power the gears groaning to turn the millstone in the belly of the two-story mill.

The broken and abandoned artifacts gave Tecumseh pause. Had this been the village of Chief Watcher and his wife, Hope? He could distinguish no ancient white sycamore about—the landmark described in the tales of their storytellers. "This must not be the place. Let us rest for the night," Tecumseh said in a low voice as if he might awaken the very woods that had lapsed into its evening repose. Indeed, the only Indians living there were in the memory of the white settlers who had moved onto the old Delaware tribal land. That was what the warrior party thought, but all was not as it appeared.

The air moving about them carried a heavy perfume upon it in the last low light before night. Weary, without making a sound, the searchers lay down upon Mother Earth within the ruins of her children. They did not dare chance a fire for warmth or cooking because they were only a whisper away from the two nearby settler cabins they had carefully avoided. Tired from a long day of traveling, the warriors ate strips of buffalo jerky to quiet their rumbling bellies. Soon, they were asleep; that is, all were asleep except Back Hawk, who was to keep guard.

As the night deepened, Lieutenant Black Hawk began to suspect that they really were in the old Delaware camp, when he saw a ghostly white tree rise up to meet the full moon through an opening in the woods. Nestled at the foot of the luminescent giant, wild flowers, bathing in dew diamonds, created a huge living bouquet—one that Black Hawk would love to take home to his Singing Bird, as he often did after a ramble in the woods. A flower pleased his young wife more than any other treasure he could give her. "These blossoms are," he vowed, "a wonder in the wilderness that Singing Bird must someday see."

Midnight now, the rest of the band slept on, while Black Hawk sat and stared out of his blanket cocoon into the scene below. He wished with all his heart that Singing Bird could be with him that night. Presently, he tunneled his attention upon the great towering tree itself. Was that a flicker of light coming from the wide split in the base? "Something in there is moving," he thought. A shadow passed over him; and, at once, he leaped silently to his feet. "What was that?" His heart raced in his chest. Deeply religious, he beseeched his guardian spirit to protect him. Quickly, he scanned the campsite around him. Nothing was stirring, not even a breeze. He stood motionless a little longer and then eased back into his blanket. "A simple shadow and I quiver like a woman," he scolded himself. For a few moments, all was quiet. Black Hawk took a deep breath and, with half-closed eyes, let his body rest, although he was far from sleep. He was softly patting his feet on the ground when he felt something touch his chest. Fear surged through him even more strongly this time as his eyes flew wide open. For a moment, he could not move because another pair of eyes—yellow eyes—loomed out of the face of the great blue-black hawk now sitting calmly upon him.

"Excuse me," the bird said.

Black Hawk shook violently but could not move a voluntary muscle from the spot where he sat. Remembering the sacred totems in his medicine bag, he could only pray that his Manito protector was with him.

"Sorry to awaken you, my brother," the hawk went on, "but I wonder if you might help me?"

Black Hawk swallowed hard and tried to speak, but no words came.

"There, there. Don't be afraid of me," the bird went on. "I am only a small black bird and you are the brave Black Hawk, war leader of the Sauk nation. How could I possibly scare you? You can't be afraid of anything."

Black Hawk gulped, closed his eyes, and opened them. The bird was still there—still talking.

"It is just, you see, that I am looking for a new spirit. It seems that the one that first enchanted me is fading, and I am about to be shut out of the circle of magic in these woods. I have been losing my powers for some weeks now and I am looking—everywhere—for a new spirit to re-enchant me."

"Oh!" Black Hawk reassured himself silently, sarcastically. "Is that all? What a nightmare! I am sure that I am dreaming; that I have fallen asleep on watch." He was not dreaming; he was not asleep.

"Oh, no; I'm quite real," the hawk went on as if he could read the young brave's mind. "I was wondering, Sir, whether you would share your spirit with me. I should like your spirit, in particular, because you are brave and strong. I want to be like that—invincible."

"What a curious request," Black Hawk murmured. "This reminds me of a vision in a spirit quest, but I am indeed not on such a search."

The bird was growing quite bold by now: "I was just wondering whether you might like to come down where it's warm inside the sycamore, where we can talk in the light."

"Could this be happening?" Black Hawk thought in disbelief. "No, it is only a vision. It has to be a dream." He closed his eyes for a moment and then reopened them, fully expecting the hawk to be gone. The bird was still there.

"Hmm," he whispered. "Maybe I am asleep. What can it hurt to follow this bird, just for a little way?" After all, the old legend about an enchanted owl that lived in a sycamore—a legacy from the famous old Delaware chieftain, Watcher, intrigued the young Indian. Even more, he wanted to get closer to the comforter of flowers, which covered the bed of the forest. Placing the bird on his shoulder, Black Hawk crept stealthily away from his sleeping companions and down toward the vision that he still thought might be a dream.

An arbor of blackberry brambles through which the Indian followed the hawk into the clearing made a trellis for the vining moonflowers and morning glories. Of course, the morning glories were sleeping, now that the sun had gone to bed; but the white moonflowers were quite awake. Their blooms were as big as any squash blossoms that Black Hawk had ever seen. Their nocturnal beauty spellbound him. On and on the two walked through fathoms of woods flowers until they came to the glistening tree. Warmed by the tiniest of campfires, the two were inside its trunk, out of the damp, after a moment of magic.

"Your fire is little more than an ember, Brother Hawk," the Indian said, with wonder in his voice. "Still, it gives off as much heat as a blazing log,"

"'Tis not just any fire, mind you," the bird answered. "It is the eternal fire of Hope."

"Of hope?" Black Hawk did not understand the meaning of the hawk's symbolic words.

"Hmm. You don't know a whole lot about this place, do you?" the bird asked. Then, looking up to a perch above them, he summoned the old Protector. "Watcher, my friend; are you awake? We have a guest!"

That was the beginning of a long night of story telling, feasting and sharing of kindred spirits. Watcher told Black Hawk the legend of Grandfather Watcher and his wife, Hope, with her constant fire. "I was named for Chief Watcher of the Delaware tribe. His wife, Hope, kept her campfire burning constantly so that wayfarers could find their way to their camp for food and rest. They were kind to all men and beasts. When they passed on, they left me in charge of the task."

The three ate from an iron Dutch oven in which a conjured frontier meat stew fed the Indian's body and soul. Both the creature and the spiritual comforts abiding in this secret place visibly touched Black Hawk.

Sometime during the evening, Black Hawk shared some secret misgivings about Tecumseh's savage tactics in fighting the white man. "I want to defend my homeland, but there must be a more civilized way." With that confession, and in that instant, the seed of peace sprouted in Black Hawk's heart.

And, perhaps, the most serendipitous part of the evening for the low-spir-
ited black bird was when Black Sparrow Hawk cordially agreed to leave a little
of himself behind to enchant the hawk. From his medicine bag, the Indian
took a pinch of red ochre powder, spat into it to make a paste, and painted the
hawk's beak. "We now share the same spirit. We are truly brothers."

The thankful hawk trembled as he felt the strength-giving life force of the
Indian's essence enter his soul. A few moments of understanding passed
between them. Presently, the conversation resumed. "Someday I will return,"
the Indian said. "I will bring my wife to touch for herself the flowers of this
forest.

"But now, dawn will soon break. I must go."

Black Hawk—the brave, the bold, and the better man for the coming—
returned to the warriors, who were just waking in the ruins.

"A quiet night," he reported to Tecumseh, while the leader rubbed the sleep
from his eyes.

Looking around at the artifacts left by the Delaware, Tecumseh said,
"Anyone can see they are gone. Nobody lives here. Let us abandon this mission
and return to our villages."[1]

[1]David D. Banta, History of Johnson County, Indiana. Chicago: Brant and
Fuller, 1888: "In 1830 there still lingered within the bounds of the State two
tribes of Indians, whose growing indolence, intemperate habits, dependence
upon their neighbors for the bread of life, diminished prospects of living by
the chase, continued perpetration of murders and other outrages of dangerous
precedent, primitive ignorance and unrestrained exhibitions of savage cus-
toms before the children of the settlers, combined to make them subjects for a
more rigid government. The removal of the Indians west of the Mississippi was
a melancholy but necessary duty. The time having arrived for the emigration
of the Potawatomie, according to the stipulations contained in their treaty
with the United States, they evinced that reluctance common among aborigi-
nal tribes on leaving the homes of their childhood and the graves of their
ancestors. Love of country is a principle planted in the bosoms of all
humankind....Color and shades of complexion have nothing to do with the
heart's best, warmest emotions."

*   *   *

So now, in the fullness of time, an old Black Hawk had kept his pledge to
return to show Singing Bird the loveliest place he had known. How was Sparrow
to know that it was he in the woods and that he posed no serious threat?

"But where are we going?" Singing Bird had asked
Black Hawk for the tenth time during the last few days.

Chapter 6

Black Hawk and Singing Bird

To further set the stage for the world and times in which Hamlet's odyssey took place, let me digress for a couple of chapters to tell you more about the Sauk Indian, Black Hawk and his wife, Singing Bird. Hamlet would have wanted me to tell you about them, in depth; so that you will more easily understand the part they played in both his life and those of his contemporaries.

The week before Black Hawk and Singing Bird embarked on their trip to Indiana had been busy...

"But where are we going?" Singing Bird asked Black Hawk for the tenth time during the last few days. Each time, he had only answered that they were going on a trip.

"Hunting," he said, now. "Just the two of us."

"Hunting?" In her mind, Singing Bird knew they were too old to be going on a hunting trip by themselves; but, in her heart, she also knew that this was important to her timeworn husband. Famous in his old age, all who knew him respected him. She would follow him anywhere, even if it were just for the adventure of it. Black Hawk was not like most of the warriors in his tribe—not at all. He had married Singing Bird when they were both very young and had remained true to only her all his life. Many of the Fox and Sauk warriors had several wives—to boast their prowess in war. Chief Black Hawk loved Singing Bird, alone.

Now, while she loaded the travois with blankets and food supplies, the old wife reflected upon his life. They had not always lived in the comfortable lodge in which the family now resided. At times, they had lived on the lam. Her husband had become famous fighting for the right to be free to live on his own land. He had won that right, which you will see later; but he had changed a little along the way. To the great wonder of many of their friends, not to mention herself, Black Hawk had even put furnishings like those of the white people into their home. Who was this man so respected in the autumn of his life by both white men and the Original Native Americans?

Black Sparrow Hawk, Ma-ka-tai-me-she-kia-kiah, was known to his friends as Black-Big-Chest. He still had a muscular torso in his senior years, but his face was thin with a sharp nose and hollow cheeks. His back was straight as an arrow, gained from a lifetime of standing proud, even though he stood only five feet and four inches tall. Head shaved, he wore a bushy scalp lock of animal hair. His ancestors had migrated from Canada to Wisconsin and he was a member of the Thunder Clan.

Singing Bird, Asshewaqua in the Algonquin language, had known him long before he became a shaman—a medicine man—at the age of nineteen. Both born in 1767, they grew up side by side in Saukenak, a village at the mouth of the Rock River in Illinois. By the time she was ten, the slender copper-skinned girl had her heart set on someday marrying Black Hawk, who was also her best friend. All too soon, the warring ways of the Eastern Woodland tribes had changed the boy, her boy-next-door, into a warrior. He was already beginning to love to wage war by the time he was 15, as did most boys that age. A couple of years later, after a skirmish with a neighboring tribe, the seventeen-year-old brave had ridden into Saukenak and stopped before a group of girls with whom his beautiful Singing Bird was sewing. They were horrified at the triumphant look that came out of wild eyes as the proud young Black Hawk held up the scalp of an Osage Indian. Blood stained his arms and chest, and a thick red paste of it covered the horse he rode. He had scalped his first man, the trophy of which he now boasted before the village maidens.

One day, soon after that, all the men and boys met together for a powwow. Led by Black Hawk's own father, Chief Pyesa, keeper of the tribal medicine, the council planned an attack on the Cherokee, a tribe who had been natural enemies of the Sauk and Fox tribe for many years. War, typically, was a favorite pastime of the indigenous Indian tribes. It was, in fact, a way of life.

On the morning of the attack, Black Hawk rode beside his father as they crept from the darkness of a timberline onto the edge of an open prairie. In the distance, it appeared that the sleeping Cherokee camp was just beginning to stir. "How foolish they are," Black Hawk thought, "to expose themselves out in the open."

He started to say so to his father when all at once the grasses between them and the camp came alive with shadows. There was one lone shriek and then a cacophony of war whoops, which sounded like a thousand screaming owls. Cherokee arrows tore through the veil of darkness. The enemy had lain in wait; they had set a trap. The Fox and Sauk fell into one of the oldest tricks of warfare—an ambush. Some of the stunned warriors spun their horses around to take cover in the woods. For others, it was too late. The deadly, speeding arrowheads had reached their targets. Black Hawk felt his father fall against him and heave a last mortal breath before falling from his horse onto the ground. Chief Pyesa was dead. Instinct alone guided the grief-stricken lad back into the woods and out of harm's way. He watched the fray through tears of a child but became a man that morning. He vowed, immediately, to take his father's place as a healer. He did not go back to war for five winters—years in which he spent his time studying the dark magic of incantations and potions to become a medicine man.

Perhaps his father's death made Black Hawk yearn for peace and later reject the efforts of Tecumseh. He had seen his father killed by the Cherokee. Later, he had seen Tecumseh killed by white soldiers. Those fight-to-the-death ways were too savage for him. Although he still believed in fighting for Indian rights, Black Hawk had begun to see that the world of the Original Native American was changing; that, indeed, all things change as long as life goes on. Change is as sure as the sunrise, and the composure with which one met that truth was the deciding factor in whether mortal man would live or perish. If anyone ever truly accepted change as a way of life, it was to be Black Hawk, before his life was over.

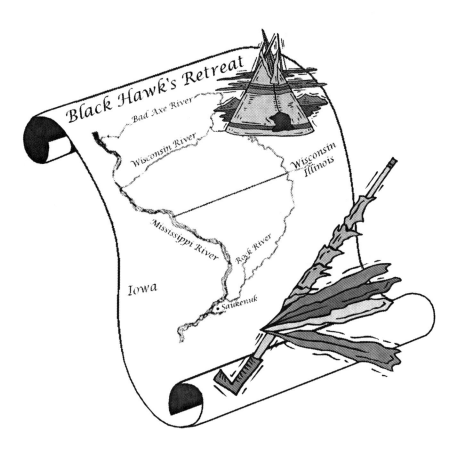

CHAPTER 7

THE BAD AXE RIVER

Hamlet had heard of the famous Delaware chief from his friends at the artist's colony in Indianapolis. Even though he had never fought in a war, he was the exception. Veterans loved to reminisce about battles in which they had fought in the various early wars. He actually had come to think of Black Hawk as a sort of folk hero. He would have found it fascinating that Black Hawk had been in Shane's very woods. Funny, how the lives of others can indirectly affect one's own.

Now, Black Hawk himself was a bit anxious about the trip to the wildflower woods of Indiana, but he had always known that somehow, someday, he would give this love gift to his Singing Bird. He had meant to take the journey when they were a bit younger; could not believe how fugitive life had been.

Would all the beauty—the magic—still be there? Black Hawk had good-humoredly decided to call this a hunting trip. True, it would be a hunting trip for he would have to find that lovely wildflower woods again, and slay a rabbit or two for fresh meat. The latter, in itself, would turn out to be the larger challenge; because Black Hawk had never been a good hunter. He had been much better at gathering—gathering herbal medicines, gathering followers.

Nonetheless, the time had come to celebrate the joy of dreams that had come to fruition in a man's life. He had learned to accept change and come to know serenity in his lifetime. "Surely, I have faced the demon War for the last time. I feel at peace with the world, now," he thought. "It is a good time to celebrate life." He no longer finished the thought when his heart felt a pang at the ever-present memory of the last great resistance of his fellow Sauk tribes-men—the Battle at Bad Axe.

"Why can't I forget the hard times and just know peace?" He turned the question over in his mind. 'Peace'. That word, that feeling, was new to his way of life. The beginning of the end of his years at war occurred four years earlier, when a bad thing happened at the Bad Axe River in the far northern reaches of the Indiana Territory—Wisconsin.

Black Hawk felt that he had been fighting all his life; but, now, he remembered just two days of it...

Two Days in June

June 1832. The white man was the Fox and Sauk enemy that June, not their old sparring tribe, the Cherokee.

It was the time of President Andrew Jackson. All out warfare between Black Hawk's followers and the U.S. Militia had been raging all around the Wisconsin River for months. After winning a few battles against the Army, the Fox and Sauk were on the run. Now, burned out of their villages, the Indian families fled the onslaught of the Army, just to stay alive. On and on the soldiers came, bent on killing the natives, not merely chasing them off the lands east of the Mississippi River.

There were nearly 2,000 Indians, of all ages, in the band, with only one hope left: to get across the Wisconsin River and travel overland to the Bad Axe River, which led to the Mississippi. Not long ago, the government promised them safety on the other side of that wide old river that divided the continent, east from west.

The pursuing militia found the tribe's trail easy to track. Littering the ground between the Wisconsin and Bad Axe rivers were pots, blankets and tools, which they had abandoned to lighten their loads so they could carry their canoes—their only means of escape. Along the trail, the militiamen found dozens of devastated Indians, mostly old people and children, who were suffering from starvation. Some of them were already dead—the rest the soldiers killed: President Jackson's orders. The days wore on, each more desperate than the one before.

Late one stormy evening the Sauk band reached the Banks of the Bad Axe. Thunder rolled down the hillsides and across the bottomland to make the enemy behind them sound like three times the number that actually rode. Lightning cracked like gunshots on the heels of the colliding clouds as the soldiers approached the rear guard of Black Hawk's braves. While most of the band had managed to cross to the far side of the Bad Axe, their heroes—the warriors—stood fast, preparing to fight the militia in a steady, cold rain. Like wounded animals, the Indians screeched terrifying war cries and turned their horses around to defend themselves. They looked hideous in the fading light with war paint swimming in rivulets down their faces to become ghoulish masks. The sudden din caused fear to sweep through the ranks of soldiers, as well as their captains. They stopped where they were—not 300 yards from the Sauk line. Not a man moved. This unusual maneuver by the Army was an unexpected turn of events to which Black Hawk quickly responded. He held up his feathered coup stick, and all became momentarily quiet.

Almost completely dark, by now, the driving rain was like a wall between the exhausted men on both sides of the fray. Slowly, a solitary officer moved his horse a few steps out in front of the troops and then paused to assess the mood of the Indian war chief. Black Hawk ceremoniously lowered his battle pole to rest on the ground and sat expressionless, as only a Native American can, at those times when there are no words. Both sides knew there would be no more fighting that day. The cavalry gingerly eased back into the woods to make camp and reconnoiter. During the night, Black Hawk and his remaining followers slipped across the river. The pursuers, too, must have been desperate for rest.

In the darkness of early morning, the Sauk and Fox families were quietly climbing into canoes when one of the disheartened warriors took it upon himself to offer surrender. A stunned Black Hawk watched as the pitiful man walked out into the river and raised his hands to show he had no weapon. In his own language, the desperate Indian pleaded, "Hear me! See the condition of our people! All we want is to stop long enough to feed our babies and women! We will travel peacefully downriver to cross the Mississippi. We are finished. The land is yours!"

The sudden invocation in the predawn alarmed the privates standing guard along the opposite bank. Not able to understand Algonquin, an already nervous sharpshooter took a single rifle shot. It cracked and reverberated in the still morning, while the half-crazed brave fell dead in the water. All hope for allowing the Indians to cross the Mississippi was gone. The sound of the shot brought the officers, indeed the entire command, out of their sleep and to their feet. Blind bullets from among some of them peppered the air, while Black Hawk quickly gathered his people into their canoes and raced down the river.

The swift crafts soon outdistanced the Army on horseback. It was a desperate chase, but the Indians reached the confluence of the Mississippi before day's end.

Barely able to paddle, Black Hawk's people could not have crossed the muddy old river without a night of rest. They quietly disembarked and, carrying their canoes, faded into the nearby woods on the eastern bank of the Mississippi. They made a cold camp where the aged, the children, and the women quickly fell into slumber. They had no food to cook, even if they had chanced a campfire. Some of the braves were beginning to drift off to get a few hours of sleep, when a scout ran into camp with bad news. The Sioux on the western side of the Mississippi lay in wait to kill Black Hawk's people. By now, on the opposite bank of the Bad Axe, the militiamen were starting their camp-fires for the night. As well, an American steamer called the Warrior had descended the river with reinforcements and dropped anchor as the sun went down upon a hopeless situation. The Fox and Sauk were in a tight spot.

Black Hawk immediately called a council meeting for the men, in which he and his good friend, the Winnebago, White Cloud, suggested breaking into small groups to travel north. There, they could hide out in the Winnebago villages among White Cloud's people. Most of their number were against this idea and asked Black Hawk if he, himself, would attempt surrender that very night. They insisted that he ask the Americans for safety against the Sioux while they crossed the mighty river to the Indian Territory. They argued that, after all, the white government had once promised them land west of the Mississippi. With little confidence that the white men would protect them against the Sioux, Black Hawk agreed to try one more time for peace.

In the moonlight, with his warriors flanking him, the chief tied a piece of white deerskin to the top of his coup stick and held it up toward the heavens. For strength of courage, he closed his hand tightly around the amulet that hung from his neck and rubbed his thumb over its turquoise beads, as if they were so many prayer beads. Cautiously, the refugees left their hiding places in the trees and waded out into the river to try to surrender. The night guard on board ship had orders to shoot to kill at the first sign of Indian movement. Before Black Hawk could utter a word, the soldiers raised their guns and instantly killed several in the envoy in spite of their peace flag. Bullets and arrows flew and fell, and a massacre ensued. Black Hawk, somehow escaping harm, dove down into the water, at last, and swam to safety behind a piece of driftwood in a thicket of cattails. The soldiers retreated and the remaining Indians were able to sink back into the surrounding woods for the night. The slaughter convinced Black Hawk, more than ever, that safety waited in the north among the Winnebago or Ojibwa villages, rather than to the west across the Mississippi.

There was an uncommon quietness in the soldier camp as the sun rose the next morning. In truth, the beleaguered pursuers seemed to be taking a day of rest: "Where are the Indians going anyway?" Somewhat relieved, Black Hawk took the time to plead with his people, but few were willing to follow him. Around noon, some of the Indians were beginning their crossing. All seemed peaceful on the other side, but Black Hawk felt very uneasy about the uncommon quiet. He feared that something wasn't right, because he had believed the runner who warned them of the Sioux across the Mississippi. A little later in the afternoon, Black Hawk, White Cloud, and thirty or forty others, who were mostly members of their families, left the main band and headed north, hidden by dense forest, to the safety of friendly Indian villages.

History would show that, of the one-hundred and fifty or so who made it alive across the Mississippi that day, few survived for long. Sioux warriors tracked down and slaughtered most of them within a few weeks.

The month after the Battle of Bad Axe, anyone even vaguely associated with Black Hawk was imprisoned. Everyone took part in this roundup: U.S. Army officers and soldiers, federal agents for the various northwestern tribes, and even some Native Americans, who felt they should show their loyalty to the federal government to be safe. Everywhere, agents sought information that might help them find the still-elusive Black Hawk.

SURRENDER IN WHITE DEERSKIN

Black Hawk, White Cloud, their families, and a few friends had made it to safety on the headwaters of the La Crosse River. Late fall now, they had camped for a few days when a group of Winnebago, including White Cloud's brother, arrived to counsel them to end the fighting and surrender themselves. Initially, Black Hawk and White Cloud had rejected this advice; but when they found themselves abandoned by the small group that still followed them, both relented. Black Hawk, White Cloud, and the rest traveled downstream to a Winnebago village and remained there for a number of days while preparing to surrender. With the army and its allies scouring the countryside for them, Black Hawk and his people recovered their strength and waited, while some Winnebago women made resplendent new suits of white deerskin for the surrender. Soon, the remnant braves of Black Hawk's band rode out of the Winnebago village and surrendered to the Indian agent, Joseph Street, at a town called Prairie Dog.

On a hot, dog day afternoon, Black Sparrow Hawk became their prisoner. He was old, even then—he was 65; but he faced the white soldiers with courage, as they led his few men, including his sons, out of Prairie Dog. Family unity ran deep in this heroic Sauk family. The defeated champion felt a pang of sympathy for Singing Bird, for he knew it would be a long, long time before he could care for her needs again—if at all.

By that night, Singing Bird knew by intuition that her husband faced great tribulation but that he was alive. For hours, she had looked to the South for it was in that direction that river husband waited for the worst. Late that afternoon, a truth had fallen upon her as she watched a sundog form in the great blue expanse before her. She dropped to the ground and with raised hands thanked Creator for sparing the lives of her husband and sons.

As Black Hawk's captors led him away to Fortress Monroe, Virginia, he was not afraid. A voice deep within him said, "Don't be afraid of the future. If you must fear anything, let it be that there will be no change. For when life stops changing, the whole of nature will perish."

PRISON ON WHEELS

President Jackson received the three at his very door and ordered his men to parade Black Hawk and his sons around the eastern cities as spoils of war. The president, this great white chief of the invaders, was wise beyond many of his subordinates, because he saw in Black Hawk a chance to reach the Original Natives through one of their own. He arranged for government officials to take the chief on a tour of the cities, army forts, and gun factories of the "new" Americans. Black Hawk saw that fighting was useless when railroads and steamers could always bring more troops of soldiers. Everywhere on the tour, the train stations were crowded with people trying to get a glimpse of the chief. The only truly sad and embarrassing departure from the President's good intentions was that the military took the old Sauk chief about in chains, to suffer the jeers of the curious onlookers, who more out of fear than common sense taunted the old native in Indian skins. They found it odd that he wore an English-style hat.

Upon Black Hawk's release, he promised not to make war again; but he was not ashamed about fighting to protect his lands. "I am a man and you are another," he told President Jackson. "...my homeland was a beautiful country. I loved my towns, my cornfields, and my people. I fought for it. It is now yours. Keep it as we did."

The truth was that he realized there were too many whites to fight.

Black Hawk returned to Iowa to live in a small cabin with Singing Bird on the beautiful Des Moines River. Soon, he furnished their home like those of the white people and taught peace to his brothers after the time of strife. He was a medicine man through it all, and many revered him and followed his pattern.

For most men, the return home after imprisonment would have been for good, but the curious Black Hawk was an exception. He truly transformed between the years of the Black Hawk War and his return from prison. He loved the Indian way, but he had room in his heart for an appreciation of the way of life he had seen in the East.

Black Hawk had brought a beautifully tanned
deerskin for his wife to record pictographs of
their trip to the wildflower woods.

CHAPTER 8

THE DEERSKIN STORY ROBE

Hamlet, like everyone else in the Riley Mill community, could not have known just how much that man, Black Hawk, figured into the discovery of his sister's absence. Indeed, he would never really know, but fate had indirectly carried the Indian's moccasins into Hamlet's world.

Black Hawk's arrow sped by his target—a rabbit for Singing Bird's stew. The poor creature zigzagged as fast as it could to get back into the bull thistles and wild roses in the depths of the darkening woods. "Auk!" the Indian cried with a defeated expression in his voice. "Fresh meat would have been good tonight! We will have to settle for Singing Bird's good hot woods stew. I think I smell it simmering over her fire up in the ruins."

It was a fact: he had never been the best of shots. He had had to depend upon snares to provide meat for the family table. Of the two most basic pursuits of most Original Native Americans—hunting and gathering—Black Hawk was definitely not a hunter. As an old Sauk shaman, he was an expert gatherer of the best natural medicines that Mother Earth had to offer.

Low of spirit, he dragged his bow beside him and started toward camp. Still fussing, he complained to himself, "After all, my eyes are 69 summers old."

And, to complicate the matter, someone had been springing his traps…

Black Hawk was surprised when he walked into camp and found that Singing Bird had the travois packed and the horse tied to a sugar maple tree beside it. She was sitting on a log holding an earthen bowl of stew for him to eat. Beneath it, she held a small pine torch to keep it warm. There was no trace of her campfire left. Smiling at her husband, Singing Bird handed him his meal.

"What is this, dear? Why have you broken camp?"

"It is time to go home."

"Why do you say that?" Although taken back by his wife's quick decision to start home, Black Hawk ate hungrily, because he had not eaten since morning.

"This place," she said, "is beautiful. Such flowers I have never seen. It is a wonderful "hunting trip" that you took me on." With that, she gave him a wink.

"Well, then, why do you want to leave so soon? What about your deerskin story robe?" Black Hawk had brought a beautifully tanned deerskin for his wife to record pictographs of their trip to the wildflower woods. He had packed, as well, the powdered dyes the family kept for painting. For as long as he could remember, each winter his wife had painted story skins of their activities that year. Singing Bird was a gifted artist who loved to recreate the beauties of nature. Real wildflowers, he knew, would wither and die; but wildflowers on a deerskin painting would last forever.

"The air was dry enough today to set the dyes. It is finished." Singing Bird stooped down to take the robe from her woven-quill carrying basket, wrapped it around her shoulders, and turned around slowly for her husband to see and admire.

"Well done. The flowers look real." He walked to her side and put an arm around her shoulders. "Your hands create flora, frozen in time."

The images of the woods flowers were indelible, now—not only on deerskin but in their minds, too. Black Hawk truly had arranged for her the best bouquet of their life together—one that both of them could cherish for the rest of their lives.

"You're sure you want to leave so soon?" he asked.

Singing Bird became somber and drew the mantle down from her shoulder. "Today, the wind was talking. I heard the voices of my grandchildren calling us home, and I was lonely. It is time to go.

"Creator sent a sign, as well. He blew the clouds on a western path to point the way home."

Singing Bird looked pale and a little older as a chill caused her to tremble before her husband. Her eyes panned the tree line and darted into the woods where Black Hawk had been hunting all day. He sensed her uneasiness.

"You are wise to note Creator's signs," he said, and gulped down his last bit of stew. "The signs are with me, too. This wood does not want to feed us. I catch nothing in my traps or with my bow."

"Husband," she whispered, "It is almost too quiet in the woods tonight. I have an ill feeling."

Without another word, under the cover of darkness, Black Hawk quietly strapped the sled to his unshod Indian pony and led the beast and his wife from the wildflower wilderness.

CHAPTER 9

HAMLET'S OTHER LIFE

Grandmother Sparrow lay wounded on the forest floor, Black Hawk and Singing Bird were on their way home, and Grandfather Hamlet was awake in the dark in his son's cabin loft.

Squirrels scampered across the roof above him on their way home from a day of gathering weed seeds to supplement their winter hickory nuts and acorns. Hamlet turned in his bed unable to sleep. Listening to the rain on the roof above him, to suit his old soul, he was lost in thought.

"Could that curious little brown creature really be my sister?" Hamlet turned the question repeatedly in his mind. For sure, he wanted to find out.

Even before the O'Sheas invited the Shuck's for a picnic, Hamlet decided to stay for a visit at Samuel and Abigail's for a few days. His family of friends in the community of artisans, where he lived in Indianapolis, would watch his weaver's shop for him. The weary Hamlet thought of his other life in the city for a while and finally fell asleep in the gently turning arms of time.

THE ARTIST'S COLONY

Like many of the other artisans who kept shops in the tiny new capitol, Hamlet conducted a cottage industry from his home. The group looked after each other. Evening would find them gathered in the Red Key, a neighborhood pub, where they could get hot meals and local ales, play checkers, and talk. Hamlet was not one for small talk, but he never tired of listening to the others discuss

the day's events and everything from their many arts to literature and religion.
For those who had served, the battles of the Indian wars were fought over and
over and late into the night. Sometimes, though, they coaxed Hamlet into
telling one of his famous fairy tales about pirates, Indians or a female apparition from another time. Of course, he never called them fairy tales. He told his
stories just as seriously as if they were true. The others, out of his hearing,
called them tales. "How could they not be fantasy?" they all agreed.
Nonetheless, whether he favored them with a tale or merely listened to them
talk, no gathering at the pub was complete without his presence. He was a well-
respected, integral part of the artisan community.

Hamlet had always been a quiet man, but a man whose presence kindled a
kind of energy that both attracted and infected those around him. A tall, well-
built man, he was an impressive figure with dense blond hair, sprinkled with
white, which fell in ringlets about his head and far down onto his shoulders.
His face was half hidden behind a great, silky beard and moustache, so that a
cursive description of his facial features could hardly be given; that is, until one
saw his graphic blue eyes. They were not the faded blue eyes that so often stare
out of the lackluster of society, but dancing, sparkling morning glories, striated
with color and fathoms deep. His were talking eyes that often spoke louder
than words.

Because they saw each other routinely, many of his everyday friends were
probably closer to him than his own family. In fact, his kin knew little of his
affairs or of him. Hamlet preferred living in town where he could be around
other artists, share his talents, and meet new people—he was always on the
lookout for anyone named Shuck. One of his favorite diversions from the nor-
mal routine was riding out into the countryside along the wilderness roads and
through the deep woods of those early days. Several times a year, these trips
took him to visit his son on the farm down in the Riley Mill community. On
his getaways, the solitude of the quiet country invited his thoughts to ramble
freely, while great adventures and introspective thoughts crawled through his
creative mind.

HOPE THE SIZE OF A FIREFLY

Now, the ride down to the farm this time had not been leisurely. Samuel had
ridden his horse to Indianapolis to get Hamlet because of the mystery of the
matching pendants; and both rode like the wind to get back to the farm. This
trip had been different, had been a real new adventure—not one conjured

from his past. The new development of the silver pieces held a glimmer of hope the size of a firefly that the woman, Sparrow, knew who his parents were.

Hamlet's grandson, Jon, had always loved his visits. Even though his grandfather appeared stern and loved to chatter, he had gentle, fetching eyes and his penchant for storytelling was especially enticing to children. During his visits, Hamlet nearly always took the boy down to the creek for private, noontime picnics and sessions of story telling. Jon had learned to love and look forward to his grandfather's company.

This was Hamlet's first visit to Sugar Creek in almost two years. In fact, he had never seen Jon's child—his great grandson, John Clay, or the new baby. He had been very busy. Indianapolis was growing larger by the day and along with the new inhabitants came new business. The tapestries from his looms were among the best in America. New artists clamored to study under him, because he was rather famous in the trade.

Allow me to digress for a moment.

Over the years, he had taken in more than a few students who showed promise at the loom—he had never forgotten the kindly master weaver who had taught him to weave at the monastery in St. Augustine. Hamlet was glad to have novices, because, in addition to helping him produce simple, routine woven goods, he was, in a sense, repaying Brother Hector for teaching him. And to his delight, every once in a while a student came along with great talent and stayed with him for a period of years as an apprentice, gleaning all he could from Hamlet's genius.

More and more clients commissioned his creations—some coming from as far as the old cities on the east coast—Savannah, Baltimore and Boston. He was, as a matter of course, becoming wealthy beyond any standard he had ever thought of attaining. However, for all his success, Hamlet's meager ways did not change. At day's end, he simply dropped off his bag of earnings at a little bank on his way to the Red Key, keeping only enough money for food and supplies. He lived so frugally, in fact, that his poorer friends in their less lucrative endeavors never even thought of him as being any better off than they were. Never once, did anyone ask him for a loan. Perhaps, none of them realized the monetary value of his tapestries, because their interests lay mainly in the excellence of his work.

None of Hamlet's fame mattered to his land-tied relatives; they hardly knew of it.

Abigail's Kitchen

Abigail Shuck stood at her big oak kitchen table over a pewter water bowl peeling potatoes to take to the picnic at the O'Sheas. Hamlet played with John Clay across from her, while he finished a second cup of coffee. A wooden spoon was the object of the child's fascination, just now, as he tap-tapped it on the table-top. It was a warm and cozy room as the smell of fresh baked bread filled every corner and the flames in the fireplace crackled in the cool, early morning. Sun streamed through the east window to promise a beautiful day in the after rain. Little John Clay had spent the night with his Granny, because he had been sound asleep when the family got back late from the strange, stormy evening in their neighbor's wood. Jon and Jesse, you see, lived just across the pasture in Grandfather Hamlet's old cabin.

It had been a long time since Hamlet sat in a kitchen bouncing a baby on his knee and watching a woman cook. Hamlet thought how much the baby reminded him of his own son, Samuel, when he was young. Moreover, he thought about Anna, his dear wife, who died so soon after Samuel was born. That was many years ago, but he still saw and felt her in his dreams and day-dreams. In the long years since, he had never found another he wanted for his wife.

His fellow artists were his companions, his weaving was his work, and Samuel's family was the only relation he had—he thought, until now, that a twin sister had seemingly turned up. He had always regretted not having known who his father was; but now that the pendants had magically opened, he, at least, had a clue. His father, most likely, was Herr Johann von Shuck from the Schwarzwald in Germany; and his mother was Gertrude, according to the inscription he found in his watch fob. The engraving read:

Clovis Shuck, twin, born October 31st, 1789
Stolen by fairy pirates, November 1st, 1791
Son of Gertrude and Johann von Shuck,
Feldberg Mountain, the Black Forest, Germany

Now, more than ever, Hamlet wanted to know everything about them. He wanted to talk to Sparrow to see what she remembered, if anything.

Abigail was glad to have some quiet time with her father-in-law. This may have been the first time since she and Samuel married that she was completely alone with the beloved old man whom her husband adored. She knew so little of him—only that when Samuel was only 18, his father had turned the farm over to him. He had taken up residence in Indianapolis where he could make a better living and return to his true vocation: weaving.

"Father Shuck," she now broke the silence. "So, how did you end up here in Indiana? I know Samuel was born in Georgia, but I never knew how you got this far north."

"Ha! Well," Hamlet said. "You've read my mind. In fact, I was thinking about that very thing."

"You were?" Abigail asked gaily. "Isn't that funny? Great minds run in the same channel, you know!"

"Oh," he laughed. "I don't know how great my mind is; but it seems the older I get the more I remember about the old days. It happens to *old* people, Abigail."

"Grandfather! You're not so very *old*," she teased him back.

Hamlet gave a warm smile and said, "Well, anyway, Samuel was just a little thing when we came to Indiana. I guess we left Georgia because his mother died and it seemed like the thing to do. There was nothing really left there for us, and I was young enough that I wanted to explore the country that was just beginning to open up."

"Like so many others," Abigail commented.

"I suppose so," he said. "Actually, at first, I traveled with a sort of Indian guide—a friend of mine from the town where we lived. His name was White Panther.

"He took us through a narrow mountain passage, which the Cherokee often used in the northwest corner of Georgia, and up the winding Tennessee River to a natural passage through the mountains he called Cumberland Gap.

"Actually, come to think of it, I believe it lies at the junction of Kentucky, Virginia and Tennessee. White Panther took us up on a high peak above it and pointed out mountains rising in all three states."

"That sounds like a hard trip to make with a baby," Abigail pointed out.

"Oh, it was," Hamlet agreed. "That's some rugged country to navigate; but beautiful, nonetheless. The Cumberland Plateau is as flat as this tabletop in some places; in others, mountains mushroom and tower for long stretches along the way. Rivers and streams carve out spectacular canyons, which are draped with waterfalls and spanned by stone arches."

"That sounds beautiful."

"That it was: beautiful, but rugged." He pondered a moment and then continued.

"Well, for the next couple of years, we just worked our way across Kentucky on Boone's Trace; and then we made it on up here."

Abigail was intrigued with Hamlet's recollections. "I know Samuel doesn't remember any of this. I've never heard him speak of it."

"You know," Hamlet said; "there is something that he may remember from that place, even though he was just a toddler: the cave in the gap. We spent a day there in a cave that was sacred to the Cherokee. The Indian took us to a chamber deep inside that held dozens of panther skeletons. There was a dark passage back to that room. We carried a torch to light the way; and, when we got close to the little room, ancient ghostly limestone drawings of giant panther cats loomed toward us, as though they were protecting the remains of their ancestor species.

"I wasn't prepared for such an apparition; and, thinking they were real, I jumped back for a moment. Samuel nearly choked me to death before we got past them. He was petrified!

"That White Panther laughed and laughed when he saw our reaction. He said he just forgot to tell us about the images, but I think he did it on purpose."

"I bet he did!" Abigail said with wide eyes. "Oh! My gosh! Let's ask Samuel if he remembers!"

"He may," Hamlet said. "Anyway, after that, White Panther went back to Georgia. I never knew for sure whether he was playing a joke on me."

John Clay jumped down and ran for the door chattering, "MeMe! MeMe!" His mother, Jesse, came in with the baby. She had come to help with the cooking and to see to John Clay, who always called her MeMe. He held his tiny hands up and she swept him into her free arm.

"Hello, Grandfather," Jesse said to Hamlet. "Is my son pestering you to play with him?" Jesse was a pretty young woman with long blonde curls bouncing off her shoulders. Her eyes were sky blue and sparkled in her slightly freckled face with its ready, happy smile.

"Ah! No," Hamlet said. "He's a grand little man; no trouble at all, are you little one?"

Hamlet did put on his jacket and hat, though, and went for a "walk around" to see what Samuel was busy at on such a clear, brisk morning. He had almost forgotten what the morning chores were like on a farm. He had been away from the task for a long time, now.

Samuel was tying some cornstalks into fodder shocks for the winter; and, soon, Hamlet found himself lending a hand. *Idleness was not one of his habits.*

CHAPTER 10

WAITING FOR SPARROW

Over at the O'Shea homestead, the morning was passing in a somewhat similar manner. Rose was cooking, Shane was repairing the fence around the chicken lot where a mink had tunneled in, but Grandmother Sparrow did not seem to be stirring yet. It was nearing mid-morning when Keren and Mack arrived to help prepare for the afternoon gathering of the two families. Kate bounded down from the carriage seat and trotted off to the sycamore to join her chums. *One never knew what excitement a new day would bring to the sycamore.*

"I'm surprised you're out so early," Rose said, "after such a late night."

"Actually, we did get up late and had a late breakfast," Mack said, slightly blushing.

Shane, who had come to the cabin, laughed. "The newlyweds! Soon enough, the honeymoon will be over, and you'll be up and out before daylight!"

Under Keren's frown, Mack quickly turned to a new subject. "I'm going down to Edinburgh tomorrow to look for a place to open an office. They have no doctor there: seems like a good place to start."

"Does that mean you'll be leaving the mill cabin?" Rose asked.

"Now, Rosie," Shane scolded. "You can't keep your little girl in your back-yard forever!"

"It's not so far away, Mother," Keren said. "We'll be back lots of times."

Mack chimed in, "Probably more than you'd like, once we start bringing you grand-younguns to fool with."

"Mack!" Keren admonished him. "Really! We just got married and you're all talking about babies already!"

"Well," Mack said. "I only want a dozen or so. I just had one brother to pester, and I want lots of kids to make up for it."

"Yes? And maybe you'll be adopting them! Who wants to be having babies all the time?" Keren retorted and walked back to the door and looked out. "Where's Grandmother?"

"I usually see her down in the chicken lot when I let the horses out of the barn," Shane said. "You know, she didn't even open up the chicken house. She always opens up the chicken house."

"I know," Keren said.

Rose gave Shane a puzzled look. "Now, what do you suppose she's up to? She knows your Uncle Hamlet is coming to see her this afternoon."

"I don't know what she's doing. You know when she gets an idea into her head nobody can stop her. She'll be back."

"Well," Rose said, "I just hope she's back before the Shuck's get here."

Everyone knew that Sparrow would be back when she got ready and not before.

"She's been getting out early the last week or so," Shane said. "Goes off into the woods and then comes back sometime before dark."

"Probably gathering plants," Keren said.

"Normally, I'd think so; but when she comes back, she isn't carrying her gathering baskets. Oh, well. Don't worry. I'm sure she'll be back in time to see Hamlet."

"I wouldn't be so sure of that," Rose said, almost under her breath. "She didn't seem so eager to talk to him last night."

The morning and noon hours passed with no sign of Grandmother Sparrow.

Mid-afternoon now, Samuel brought his big, new carriage up to the Shuck cabin. He had given his old one to Jon and Jesse. Today there would be a full carriage with six Shucks, plus the baby and two baskets of food. Jon and Jesse rode in the back holding the food and child, while Abigail holding John Clay nestled in between Samuel and Hamlet.

Well built of hard, new wood with extraordinary curved lines and decorative carvings, the one-horse carriage had strong springs for comfort.

"This sure is a fine trap you got here, Sam," Hamlet said. "You buy it around here?"

"No, there's a wagon maker in Corydon. His family has been in the business down there since the turn of the century, when the state was still a territory. He is a friend of John Riley's. John and I went down and ordered it, when we found out Jesse's new baby was on the way. Took the wood with us; got it from a big hickory we cut down in that east field."

"I remember that tree. It was here when you and I moved on the place. Shame to have to trade it for the carriage," Hamlet lamented.

"Yeah, I know. I cannot remember when it was not there. It took that old wagon maker four months to build it, but isn't she a beauty?"

"It sure is, Son. It sure is. I always loved the rich color of Indiana hickory wood."

Gently flicking the reins to signal the beast forward, Samuel nodded his head toward William. "When we cut the tree down, Old William, here, pulled it on down to Riley's mill to be ruffed out. Next day, Riley and I put the wood in a wagon; and William carried us on down to Corydon."

"When it was done, how'd you get it back up here?" Hamlet asked.

"Why, I rode Will back down and got it," Samuel laughed. "We felt like a couple a big dogs all the way back. I never had anything so elegant to ride in, and he never had anything so elegant to pull."

Everyone in the carriage laughed. After that, besides John Clay's chattering, there was no real conversation for the rest of the ride to the O'Shea cabin. All of them were thinking about Sparrow and Hamlet's short reunion the night before and what today might bring.

When the Shucks arrived, Shane and Mack were cleaning off the split-log table under the trees between the old sycamore and the cabin. Keren and Mack had been married there only a couple of days before in the beautiful wildflower setting. It seemed, though, that it had been more like a couple of weeks: so much had happened in the last 48 hours after the discovery of the matching pendants. When the two saw the Shucks pulling up in the new carriage, they went up to the cabin to greet them.

"Hello! Hello!" Shane welcomed them. "How's the new buggy handling? I can see why you are so proud of it. It'll hold a small regiment, won't it?"

"Yep," Samuel said, "I guess so. All of us fit in it, and there is still room on the back for a couple more."

"Keren!" Mack shouted. "Come see the new carriage! Samuel's here!"

Rose and Keren came out of the cabin to help Abigail and Jesse with the children and the basket.

The men unhitched William and took him out with the other horses in the corral behind the barn, and then walked back out to sit in the yard. John Clay ran off to the sycamore to play. In the cabin, the women fussed over the food and the new baby. Shane just happened to have a jar of dandelion wine on the table and five wooden cups, which he had made himself. He poured a round.

"A toast!" he said, lifting his cup toward Hamlet. "A toast to Clovis and Claire Shuck! May they live long and well!"

Hamlet looked around, but nowhere could he see Sparrow. He was anxious to talk to her. "Where is my sister?"

Shane really was starting to feel uneasy. The afternoon shadows were beginning to stretch long to the east, and Sparrow still had not returned from the woods. "Well, I'm not really sure. She has gone out to the woods again today. She has been spending a lot of time out there lately. But don't worry; I'm sure she'll be back just any time now." Nevertheless, something told him she would not be back for the picnic.

"What's she doing in the woods," Mack asked, "gathering plants and roots for her concoctions?"

"I wish I knew; she's beginning to worry me. Even though she is my mother, sometimes I feel I do not know her at all. Many people come to her for remedies; and then, other times, she will go to them—especially when someone is having a baby."

"And, she takes that peacock everywhere she goes;" Rose added. "It even sleeps with her in the loft in the winter."

Mack spoke up, "I noticed that she has been preoccupied lately, but I thought maybe it was just around me. I know she doesn't cotton much to my medical practice."

"You're right about that," Samuel said. "She told Abigail you ought to learn a good trade like Shane with his woodworking; that you don't know much about doctoring because you can't tell one root from another; that you can't cure anyone that way."

"I can too!" Mack laughed.

The afternoon wore on. The meal was ready, so the women spread it on the same wooden tables used for the wedding dinner and everyone ate. Night was near and still no Sparrow. Mack and Jon built a bonfire to keep away the damp. Rose and Keren-happuck brought out mats and quilts to sit on around the fire. Jon took his son to catch lightning bugs for a while and then brought him back and laid him on the quilts to sleep before the fire.

After the bonfire was lit, unbeknownst to the people sitting in the dark twilight, the fairies crept out of the sycamore to join them. The banshee, the brownie, and the nix arrived as invisible spirits; and the owl, Watcher, came as he was and perched on a low tree branch above the party. They knew, by now, that Miss Sparrow had been missing far too long into the evening.

"I think I'd better go look for her," Shane said. "She surely knew we'd be waiting for her."

The fairies, on the other hand, knew that she was not okay. "We must send for the black hawk and the ground squirrel for a full fairy council in the Enchanted Tree, nothing less," Watcher advised.

Keren-happuck still thought her grandmother would show up. "No, Dad. She is okay. She will be along after while. She is probably just not ready to talk about this yet. If I know her, she's out there, nearby, just watching us through the trees."

"You're probably right, daughter. Just a little longer," Shane said. "Uncle Hamlet, how about telling us about the mission in St. Augustine where you were raised? Samuel said that's where you learned to be a weaver."

"Yes!" everyone agreed. That was a story they wanted to hear about. Florida seemed like another, faraway world.

"Well," Hamlet hedged, "that was a long time ago. I can hardly remember."

Samuel spoke up then. "Dad, I know you never have talked much about the past, but there must be something you can remember that may tie you and Sparrow together. Won't you try?"

Hamlet poked the fire. "I wouldn't know where to begin."

"At the beginning," his daughter-in-law, Jesse, urged him. "How far back can you remember?"

Tiny sparks rose from the crackling embers. Reluctantly, Hamlet started to think back. He had never been at ease talking about his past, because he did not really know who he was. Maybe, now that the pendants had unlocked vital information about his life, he could make some sense of it.

"Well, let me think for a few moments. I'm an old man, and I haven't thought about my childhood for a very long time." In the last glimmers of twilight, he stepped out of the circle, picked up a long stick, and walked among the wildflowers—petals closed for the night and wet with dew—to collect his thoughts.

The Shucks and O'Sheas hugged the fire and spoke in low voices while they waited for Hamlet. More importantly, they all knew, including Hamlet, that they were really waiting for Sparrow.

"Hamlet saw himself standing in the sand; a pirate ship rocked in the waves just offshore."

Chapter 11

Gathering Memories

It is a good thing to revisit the playgrounds of youth. While his friends and family waited around the bonfire, Hamlet gathered memories.

The Pirate Days

Hamlet saw himself standing in the sand; a pirate ship rocked in the waves just offshore. The sun in a blue, clear sky rode the sweet wind up from the South Pacific; it warmed him just now. Even in these far reaches of his memory, Hamlet wondered whether the boat had really existed. Was it all a bad dream? No. He had spent ten years upon the sea, in all that beauty of spectacular sunsets and sunrises; yet, he never wanted to go near the ocean again.

Bittersweet memories lingered from his days with the fairy pirates. He had known that he was different, that he was not one of them. The buccaneers were a misery on the main, but they were not unkind to him. They treated him with the tenderness and affection one would shower on a puppy. He knew it was not brotherly love—not family love; he was but their toy. *But, that was another story.*

His silver pendant recorded his kidnapping, but he could not remember any of the details. Indeed, he could not have known the truth of it; but when he was two, a band of mischievous banshee fairies placed him in a bag and sold him to fairy pirates, telling them it was a piglet. Once out at sea, the betrayed, bandana-clad miscreant pirates were furious when they opened the bag to find that it held a child. Some were so enraged that they thought of throwing the boy into the sea; others were curious about the rosy-cheeked baby with ringlets of gold hair. Fortunately, the lot of them quickly lost their hearts to the child's magic smile. They named him Hamlet over the objection of some, who thought Piglet was a better name because of the way the banshees had represented him. In the end, they raised the boy they bought onboard ship beneath the Jolly Roger.

The buccaneers plundered the rich ships of the Caribbean Sea. The older the boy got, the more he longed to join the ranks of mortal man. The ghoulish, bad fairy pirates about their misdeeds grated Hamlet's young soul and caused him to become wistful and discontented. He was no longer the happy, bright "piglet" who used to amuse them. Reluctantly, when he was twelve, the pirates put him ashore. He saw himself, standing there—too old to cry, too young to be afraid.

"How can I tell these people my story about the pirates is true? Who would believe such a tale? No. It would seem like fantasy to them. I will leave that part out. Perhaps, I should begin with the mission: with real people."

The Mission Years

This is how his seven-year sojourn at the mission began:

Hamlet stood in the sands of time on the east coast of Florida. Across a shallow inlet with a coquina shell bottom, he saw a tall wooden cross. He had seen that cross rising high above the trees as the pirate ship approached the land. Large dark herons, as tall as himself, with wings that opened to twice the width of his outstretched arms, fished in the crystal clear water, through which he walked to reach land's end—his new beginning. Now, reaching that Christian landmark, he looked through stately live oaks, shrouded with hanging moss, to spy a glistening white statue standing in a grotto between the door and the roof of a tiny, vine-covered chapel. He later learned that the structure was an ancient mission church, the Nombre de Dios. He had never seen a holy relic before. The stone-carved image of a man with outstretched arms and wearing long flowing garments called to him. The likeness spoke a thousand silent welcomes. Hamlet breathed a sigh of relief and walked across a small arched footbridge, which spanned a small pond, outlined in cattails and palms. A pair of swans swam in graceful circles and looked curiously at the adolescent, brown boy.

In those silent days of quiet industry, before the sounds of progress descended upon St. Augustine, the mission grounds came slowly alive with voices of people as Hamlet walked down a wide path of finely crushed seashells. Through the old, salt-bleached trees, he now saw low buildings, made white by the salt sea spray; and people—Indians, robed men and habited nuns—going about their work in just one more day of life at the mission. On the far side of the low wall, which surrounded the entire grounds, huge wooden gates opened into the old town of St. Augustine.

In only a moment, two holy sisters discovered Hamlet, swept him into their arms, and whisked the orphan into the mission fold.

The monks took him in as a chore-boy in return for food and shelter. He lived in the back room of the weavers' trade shop for seven long years. For an orphan boy, he spent his time well; because, one day, the master weaver, Brother Hector, discovered that by watching the weavers the child had taught himself the art. Hamlet showed such great promise that the monk offered to teach him English and took him in as his private apprentice—a great honor.

Hamlet had loved his work at the weaver's art. The intricate pieces made by the gifted boy brought the highest revenue of any artist at the mission. In return for producing the valuable woven goods, the brothers excused the boy from one of his routine tasks—that of training their Creek and Seminole Indian students. This allowed him to create original designs and to make his own private garments and dry goods. He always added elaborate touches, including the Seminole Indian flavor, to his personal belongings—an indulgence he could not resist, artist-extraordinaire that he was. He was better than the Master Weaver.

Being the best weaver was not enough to fulfill the solitary young man's life. After his seven-year apprenticeship, Hamlet felt the need to go out into the world in search of his identity.

Map to Freedom

When he left the Spanish Mission at St. Augustine, Hamlet was a man with no cradle, a man with no cause, save to discover his origin. The year was 1808 and he was only 19; yet, his was an old soul, rich with history and ripe with memories and half-memories.

Hamlet was an orphan. He knew nothing of his family. He spent his childhood with pirates and his youth with missionaries. He did not belong to either way of life. His natural demeanor, as well as his physical features, exhibited none of the Spanish affinities.

In his own mind, young Shuck had come to believe that he was of German ancestry—a theory really planted by Brother Hector. Together, they had pieced together a few clues to Hamlet's past. The boy thought that his name was

Shuck and Brother Hector thought that the first tapestry Hamlet ever made looked like dancing German children. Even the silver chain and pendant Hamlet wore were German by design—the image of an edelweiss was etched into one side.

The morning he departed, a group of friends, both monks and Indian weaving students, had gathered at the gate of the mission to say good-bye. Hamlet was armed with a pouch containing a deerskin map. It was of an ancient Indian trail used by the Seminole, Creek, and other southeastern tribes. Brother Hector had actually copied it from one of the maps held at the mission to help Hamlet find his way into the northern frontier.

Brother Hector knew of a place in Northwest Georgia where a group of Germanic Moravian people had once founded a mission in an old Cherokee town. It lay at the foot of the Appalachian Mountains above the Lower Creek Indian territory. The monk had never been there, but it was at least a place for the young weaver to start his search.

Swift Weaver, a Creek student whose father was a warrior of the prestigious Wind Clan, was well familiar with the terrain over which his friend Hamlet would have to travel. He knew of a safer Creek Indian trail that Hamlet could take to get to Spring Place where the Moravians had taught the Cherokee. He drew a new route with landmarks on Brother Hector's map. Together, the three of them went over the details of the drawing.

Pointing to the map, Swift Weaver said, "Take this route. White men call it the Surveyor's Trail. It is an old Indian footpath and well worn from centuries of moccasins and animal paws. It will take you six days to come to the Suwannee, a river that flows down from the northeast. About three miles more, you will come to another trading path, which will take you north into South Georgia. It lies between two rivers—the Alapaha and the Withlacoochee. Follow that trail for a day and you will step across the Florida-Georgia border at the landmark: a field of sunken holes at the base of an age-old outcrop of jagged red rocks on three craggy knolls. One more day, and you will come to a Y. Bear left and travel in a northwesterly direction until you come to a lake, which lets out into this: he pointed to the Flint River. Follow that river for four days.

"There are Creek towns governed by mico chiefs along the banks of the rivers. Some are friendly, some not so friendly. Just stay on the main trail, which lies well inland from the rivers; you will probably not be noticed or stopped. With a Spanish rig, you will not pose a threat to them. The Creek and Seminole are allies of the Spanish."

Hamlet asked Swift Weaver whether there would be enough water for him and his animal by traveling inland.

"The land along the trail is grassy and several springs run through it," his friend told him and held up the map. "There should be no need to go to the river or stop at the Creek towns until you get to Coweta—just here," he pointed. "The trail runs right through the town, and I have relatives there. I will send a gift to the mico so that he knows you are my friend.

"You will recognize them as Creek because the braves will be wearing turkey feathers and animal skin clothing—none of the woven blouses that the Seminole and Cherokee wear."

Swift Weaver handed Hamlet the delicately carved walking stick that he had been carrying that morning. Its handle was an alligator, whose mouth held a man, waist up. The victim's head, the top of the staff, was bald and smooth and the whole stick was a sturdy twist of cypress wood. "My uncle is the chief. This stick, he will recognize: the alligator is the totem of our clan. You will be welcomed. Of course, he will expect you to trade with him. Here, take these." He handed Hamlet a handful of blue Venetian beads, which he took from his pocket. "My uncle will, perhaps, trade you some deerskin clothing for them. The climate is cooler in the mountains of the frontier.

"When you leave Coweta and cross the Chattahoochee River, you will be among the Cherokee, who people the North Georgia Mountains. They call their homeland the "enchanted land," and themselves, the "principal people." You will know them by their speech—the Iroquoian language, not the Muskogee language of the Seminole. They will dress differently, Hamlet. Many of their warriors dress like the white man and wear fabric shirts.

"Do not be afraid of the Cherokee for they are a very "civilized" sort and get along well with the white settlers. They will direct you to Spring Place if you get lost."

"This is my map to freedom," Hamlet thought to himself.

Also, in preparation for the trip, Swift Weaver helped Brother Hector and Hamlet pack food stores, a few eating utensils, and a trunk of trade goods, which were made at the mission: beads, vials of dyes, and balls of twine. Hamlet had saved considerable money, mostly gold coins, which he had hidden well away in the floor of the cart.

The time of leaving was a tender moment for them all. Hamlet was both friend and teacher to the Native Americans who learned trades at the mission. He and Swift Weaver, especially, would remember each other fondly. However, his relationship with the brothers was more like "family." Brother Hector, especially, imagined that the pangs of sorrow he felt at Hamlet's leaving were like a father's, when his son leaves home to find his destiny, perhaps never to return.

He tried to think of something wonderful and wise to say about how to accomplish such a quest as this one. However, at this moment of farewell, only the words, "I hope you find your people," escaped, as he embraced his protégé and winked back tears.

"Someday, my father...," Hamlet said to the emotional monk; but he stopped in mid sentence. A smile of embarrassment came to his face.

"I called you father, didn't I?" he said. "I'm afraid you've found me out. Sometimes I think of you as my father."

The monk smiled approvingly. "I know what you mean," he said. "I think of you as a son, too."

"Well," Hamlet continued, "what I was going to say was that someday I hope to see you again."

"God willing," Brother Hector said. "Maybe you will come back to pay your debt. Remember, you owe me a horse and wagon!"

Hamlet laughed and stepped up into the cart. With a tip of his straw hat, he smiled down at his friends and then turned forward and loosened the reins. The horse pulled away—away from the mission, away from the tall ships in the harbor. The dust rose in the trail behind them and then settled as they entered the main road that went through St. Augustine.

Hamlet turned and watched the steeple and the masts getting smaller in the distance until he could see them no more. After that, he would not look back— only forward.

Rehabilitating banshees has never been easy; re-enchanting them is nearly impossible. Only the great Oberon has the power to do it.

CHAPTER 12

THE WAY THROUGH THE WOODS

While Hamlet was reminiscing, the American Spirits had convened their council. They met in the rotunda of the tree trunk to organize a search party to find Grandmother Sparrow.

"I remember the last time we gathered here for a full fairy council," the presiding owl began. "It was when the rogue mud diver captured you, Keen."

The banshee shuddered. "That was the worst nightmare of my life!"

"I'm sure that it was," the owl consoled her. "But now, we may have another emergency, and it is every bit as serious. Miss Sparrow has surely met some disaster. Both she and her peacock seem to have just disappeared somewhere in the depths of the woods.

"Just let me ask the lot of you whether you have any ideas where she could be. Do you remember her saying anything at all that may lead us to her?"

Keen shared with them, again, the events of Sparrow's strange behavior the night before. "I feel that something is amiss in the woods that only she knows about."

The rest of the fairies racked their brains, but none could come up with an answer.

The black hawk spoke. "Several years ago, I was enchanted by a young Indian scout. That enchantment brought with it many good traits from the Indian himself. I am, for example, a very good scout. I shall conduct an aerial search through the woods to try to spy Sparrow."

"Excellent idea, Black Hawk," Watcher said. "Anyone else have any ideas what the rest of us should do?"

Perhaps the least of the spirits, Chelsea, the little striped ground squirrel, suggested in a tiny voice that the fairies should divide and cover the floor of the woods. "I cannot see above the wildflowers well enough to spy her; but fairies, such as yourselves, can flit above them easily."

The banshee was not listening. In near hysteria over her lifelong Irish soul sister, she twirled in nervous jerks about the interior of the trunk. "If you want to know what I think, it is that we should call upon the king and queen of the Faire for help!"

Pitt, although truly concerned by now, was not quite ready for that drastic a move. "No Keen! I say! Remember yourself! We should only contact the royal Oberon and Titania as a last resort. We should not ask them to intervene in human matters until every other effort is exhausted. They bestow our magical powers for a reason. Let us call upon our own resources for now."

"Oh! I know," she conceded to the brownie; "but I bet you'd feel the same way if this revolting turn of events had happened to your precious English Rose."

"Excuse me! Rose Caine O'Shea is a saint of a woman, as loving as a dove in the eaves of a church!"

"Pigeon poop!"

The nix jumped to her feet and shouted: "Now I ask you two! Is this any time to rekindle your ancient British feud?

"Brits!" the German fairy continued. "Will you ever stop scrapping? Even in America you argue!"

"Tut-tut!" scolded the owl with a loud, stern screech. "Stop this instant! All of you! We will deal with this American crisis in the American way! Now, I'm sure your royal Faire could find Sparrow; but have you no pride?"

Ashamed, the three European fairies hushed their bantering and gave Watcher their full attention.

"The search party," Watcher instructed, "will spread out in this way: first, Black Hawk, you are right: you must search from above; Pitt, you cover the west woods while Keen covers the east; Katrina, take the strip down the middle. Moreover, Chelsea, there is something you can do. Go to your kitchen and prepare a great deal of sassafras tea and hickory nut cakes. We shall all need sustenance when the search is over.

"I," the owl concluded, "shall wait here until word comes from one of you. When it does, I'll call in the rest."

Black Hawk's Sky Search

The search was on. Black Hawk flew far up above the forest to get a good view of the lay of the land, but the trees were so numerous that even his sharp eyes could not penetrate its depths. He banked his wings toward the northwest corner of the O'Shea woods and planned to zigzag left to right across the woods at a level just below the leaves. Even then, it would be difficult to see through the underbrush. Starting to descend, he caught, out of the corner of one eye, movement in the twilight.

"What's this?" Just as soon, his heart took an unexpected leap and something moved in his inner being. A power larger than life called him to that spot. "It could be Sparrow," he reasoned; but in his heart, he did not really believe that. Involuntarily, his wings dipped and glided toward a current of energy, which he could not resist. In an instant, he beheld the Sauk Indian who had re-enchanted him so many years ago when his powers faced extinction. He flew in circles above Black Hawk and Singing Bird, while trying to get a clear fix on the business below, which had drawn him to distraction whilst on the search of the old grandmother.

"Bless me! It is the Sauk Indian himself! I vow. He has kept his promise to bring his wife to the wildflower woods!

"But, what's this? It looks as though they are leaving. How curious; he didn't even visit the enchanted tree! Ah, well, she probably doesn't believe in enchantments. That would be why.

"I wonder whether I should take the time to have a word with the old man, to ask whether he has seen Sparrow. Alas, she is not with them. I believe the two old souls are better left alone.

"They are traveling with wind under their wings. The Indians are like that. They travel on fleet feet and often by night—a habit that has evolved over many years of fleeing warring tribes and the white man.

"I'll just glide down for a quick close look at my friend, Black Hawk, and then get on my way."

A sudden dive on a downward air current carried him to within three feet of Black Hawk and Singing Bird. The couple was startled that a bird came down so close to them. For Singing Bird, it was just one more omen that they should leave; but a smile came to Black Hawk's old wrinkled face; for a moment, he paused to watch the bird fly back into the forest.

"I remember," he said softly to his wife, "a dream I had when I visited this wood in my youth. In it, I shared my spirit with a black hawk."

PITT'S WEST WOOD SEARCH

Pitt pattered along an animal trail that ran through the western third of the 47-acre woods. The brownie was nervously talking up a storm, in his typical English accent, while his quick bright eyes took note of every movement on either side of him. "Poor old Miss Sparrow. My word. Where has she gotten to in the middle of the night?" Then, "Oh dear, oh dear. I have a frightful feeling the old girl has fallen upon an unfortunate turn of events."

Because he was not watching his step, the brownie tripped over the hem of his robe, repeatedly. "Oh, bother!" he fussed. "By Jove! I'm tangled up again!" Finally, he reached down and gathered up his cloak with his hands to keep from stumbling so much. What a sight he was scurrying down the winding path, skinny legs jutting out of the folds of his flowing garment and prattling like a jay. In between his chattering tirades, Pitt often called out "Miss Sparrow!" It was in vain. The brownie became less and less hopeful that he would find her as he raced through the familiar trails he'd come to know in Shane O'Shea's homestead.

KEEN'S EAST WOOD SEARCH

Keen was not having any better luck as she combed the bottoms and the creek, which ran through the eastern portion of the property. She was, by far, the most suitable fairy to search the water; because, like all banshees, she was a descendant of the fairy species, *Water Sprite*, who had risen from the fresh water springs in Ireland since time immemorial.

About half way through her assignment to cover the eastern reaches, Keen started to experience cold chills. She quivered under the chill bumps on her skin until walking became extremely difficult. A few steps more and her stiff legs stopped moving. Whether frozen with the damp, or frozen with fear, the banshee could not budge. Keen's eyes glazed over with tears; and, in a moment, she lost all sense of her surroundings. Fragile essence that she was, the sprite faded in and out of view like a firefly in the dark. Then, time stood still as she completely disappeared. Not a sound came forth from the fauna and insects, which teemed in the undergrowth and trees. Even the breeze, the voice of the forest, lay quiet.

Keen whirled through the netherworld of the fairy sphere. Queen Titania had sent a royal zephyr down to collect the ailing banshee. When the fairy regained consciousness, a band of caretaker fairies was attending to her disheveled condition. Tiny golden combs in hand, the grooming fairies were restoring her silky hair to its original luster. Bathing fairies were swabbing her skin with rose-scented fairy balm, and the wing-designer fairies were restoring the gold and ivory gossamer fans with which she flew.

"Feeling better, my dear?" Queen Titania asked Keen, while dropping a filmy new gown over the banshee's head. "You gave us quite a scare."

"Am I alive?" the banshee asked in a weak voice, not sure of her state of being. She felt dull of mind, without an ounce of energy. "How did I get here?"

"You were having a rather hard time of it out there in the earthly world," Titania comforted her. The queen gently stroked the banshee's cheek with her nurturing motherly touch.

"I was?" Keen asked. Temporary amnesia had erased her memory for the moment.

"Sleep now," Titania said, and gracefully passed her wand over the drowsy fairy. Keen closed her eyes and sank into the satin-covered eiderdown bed upon which the caretaker fairies had placed her.

"Send for the king," the queen kindly ordered. "He'll know what to say to her when she awakens."

Rehabilitating banshees has never been easy; re-enchanting them is nearly impossible. Only the great Oberon had the power to do it. The handsome fairy king stood over the banshee, whom his wife had rescued just in time.

"An instant more," he told Titania, "and she would have been completely and utterly lost to the land beyond memory. You did well, my dear, in looking after your flock."

"You flatter me, Sire; but what I did was easy compared to the task before you. I have restored her body, but you must restore her spirit. The world was so much with her that she lost her way. The Family O'Shea is not easy. Their old, rich souls are hard to harness; but they are the rarest privilege to serve."

"This banshee," he said, "young though she is, has done as well as any centuries-old Irish fairy could have done. The wee lass only need face her fears. That is all; just learn that the humans' Creator carefully lays out all the stages of development of the human family. Fear, you see, my darling queen, is a state of mind and has nothing to do with reality."

Titania was impressed, as usual, with her husband's ability to assess so quickly the crux of the problem. More of a gentle lady than a scholar, the queen wondered: "Just what is it that she is so frightened of, Oberon?"

"It's a word that only applies to creatures that walk the earth: that word is death."

"Death?" Titania echoed. "That seems like a harmless enough word. Such a tiny word. What does it mean?"

"It means, my love, that all living things on earth, each in its own time, passes on to another form of reality. That is, Titania, an elementary and completely natural process, which does not pertain to the Faire."

"Go on," the queen said.

"Humans do not realize that, in some form, they live on forever. The Benevolent Source of their being would not take the time to make them, just to toss them away like so much flotsam. He does not make mistakes and has a plan for each and every of them.

"How very extraordinary," Titania mused.

"Oh yes," Oberon further explained. "They are fashioned with great dimension and purpose. They even possess the gift to produce other humans like themselves. They call those offspring children. Humans have even made a scientific study of this ongoing process: they call it genealogy. In it, each generation, in its own less-than-a-century lifespan, gets packed up into a group. That group becomes ancestors of all the descendants; in other words, all the children, that follow."

"Less than a century?" Titania asked thoughtfully. "Time is fleet for Earth's inhabitants."

Oberon sighed heavily. "Ah! This poor banshee has an opportunity to experience her finest hour as a family fairy. If her mistress, the old Irish grandmother, passes on to another state of being, Keen could be quite useful in helping the rest of the family to adjust. She could help them to realize that it is okay for Sparrow to leave one stage of life and go on to another. It is, Dear, our task to help her prevail."

"And that, we shall!" the royal diva vowed. "What have you in mind?"

"Oh!" King Oberon replied, "We shall not have to do a thing more. Although the little Keen sleeps, she hears every word and her enchantment has been restored. When she awakens, she will be a little wiser in the ways of the world, but remember none of this."

Thin air began to twirl in the path by Sugar Creek until the faint ghost of a spirit emerged as the clear and unmistakable image of a living, breathing banshee. Shortly, Keen hovered as gracefully and resplendently as a damselfly, then she darted down to sail her course in the eastern wood.

KATRINA'S MIDDLE WOOD SEARCH

Katrina, the nix, was making great strides through the middle region of the search area. To make better time on this particular night, she spread her translucent nixie wings and flew above the sleeping wildflowers and in and out of the trees until she came to the cabin clearing where the worried families waited for Sparrow. Katie entered the yard transformed into her usual American guise—a dog. Trotting past Mack, she stopped for a pat on the head.

"Hello there, pooch," her master greeted her. "Why don't you make yourself useful and go find Grandmother Sparrow."

The fairy dog licked Mack's hands and went along her way down through the middle wood.

Shane stood up and watched Kate fade into the trees. "I believe," he said, "that I'll just go see if Mother is in her loft. It would be just like her to sneak in and we not know it. If she isn't there, I'll just have a walk down to the dock to see whether she's night fishing."

This time, Keren-happuck did not object. Her grandmother was out much later than usual. Even Hamlet, who had been lost in his memories, walked back and sat down to wait for his peculiar sister to return. It was getting late and the night air had become a little too damp for any bonfire storytelling that night.

Rose had tired of the night air and invited her guests up to the cabin for hot tea. "Let's go inside. It's getting mighty chilly out here, and we can wait just as well in the house."

"Good idea, Rose. I'm afraid the children will take cold," Abigail said. "We need to be getting home as soon as Grandmother Sparrow gets back. I know Jesse doesn't like being out too late with the baby."

The party moved inside while Shane searched the barn and loft. Presently, he stepped in the cabin door and said he was just going to pop down to the dock. Shane was carrying a gourd lantern, which he had recently made by poking holes in the soft flesh of the body and then letting it harden. The gooseneck of the fruit made a perfect handle. He took a candle from the candle box on the wall, put it in the body of the lantern, and lit it with a stick at the fireplace. Doctor Mack decided to join Shane while the rest enjoyed their hot drink. Meanwhile, Hamlet hoped that his family would not expect him to go on with his story, at least, not for that evening. No such luck.

"So, Grandfather," Jon said. "What have you been thinking about out there in the yard? You didn't think we'd forgotten, did you?"

Samuel, too, was curious to know more about his father. He had always known there were mysteries untold surrounding his own early life and that of his father. Now that he had Hamlet on the subject, he wanted him to go on; otherwise, the family story would remain a mystery for perhaps much longer.

Hamlet shuffled in his chair and took a cup of rosehip tea from Rose. He spooned a lump of maple sugar into his steaming drink and lifted it to his lips. "Well," he took a sip. "I suppose it's as good a way as another to pass the time while we wait for Mrs. O'Shea"

"Grandfather," Jon interrupted. "She's your sister, not some stranger you call 'Mrs.'"

"Ah, yes," Hamlet agreed. "It's hard to get used to that realization. I guess she is my sister; at least, it looks that way."

"So then," Samuel pressed Hamlet. "Go ahead."

An hour ticked away while Grandfather Shuck spoke of his adventures with a Cherokee Indian in the North Georgia Mountains. His voice wrote invisible words on the four walls of the old storybook cabin.

Smiley's Mill Photo Album

SMILEY'S MILL

Major John Smiley, born in Nelson County, Ky. in 1781, came north through Washington County, In., in search of a mill site. He settled for a place on Sugar Creek in Needham Twp. which is now 5 miles south east of Franklin on the Greensburg Road, at the intersection of 700 E. Here he built a saw and grist mill, and just northeast of the mill, Smiley built his cabin. At this cabin, following the March 8, 1823 elections, the organization of the county took place. Judge William Watson Wick held the first court in the Smiley cabin, on October 16, 1823. John Smiley was the first sheriff of Johnson County.

The present channel for Sugar Creek, just south of Camp Comfort to the Smiley's Mill Bridge is the mill race. The bayou, or old bed of the creek, is on the east side of the bridge, looking north. The Smiley dam was made of logs. The present dam, built in the 1930's by the W P A, under the supervision of Barnett Fox, was built of enormous beams and huge boulders.

The Smileys' Mill brick school was located just north of the cemetery, and east of John Smiley's cabin, in a grove of walnut trees. John Smiley died in 1854 and is buried in the Smiley cemetery.

The mill continued to be operated by members of the Smiley family until after the turn of the century. William Smileys' Amity Mill copper stencil, used for marking bags of flour and meal, was given to the museum by Mrs. Louis O. Johnson, and may be seen in the farm room. Dr. Robert Hougham recalled having his hair cut at the mill as a child.

Vincent Shipp lived just north of the mill and taught music- he also organized a small orchestra from his pupils.

The saw mill was removed from the grist mill near 1900, and the timbers holding the grist mill rapidly deteriated, causing the remaining building to fall into the creek in 1905.

Mr. and Mrs. Norbert Vaught have recently remodeled a barracks from Freeman Field at this site, and intend to make their home here.

School Children in front of the Smiley's Mill School. Pictures given by Laura B. Webb

Although faint, this original photo, taken by an unknown source, captures the mill on Sugar Creek from a north vantage point. It appears that the photo was taken from a small river craft sometime before Smiley's Mill fell into the current in 1905.

Smiley's Mill, ca. 1900

The Needham Township mill above helped inspire the "Sugar Creek
Anthologies of Jesse Freedom" series. Photo Source: **Nostalgia News.**
Editor: Rachael Henry, Curator, the Johnson County Historical
Museum, Franklin, Indiana, October 1, 1978, Issue No. 6, p. 12.
Permission granted.

Roof ruins after the rest of Smiley's Mill into the creek in 1905.

Schoolchildren in front of Smiley's Mill School.
Photo taken by *Laura B. Webb.*

PART THREE

HAMLET & THE CHEROKEE
BASKET MAKER

"Many rivers run against you.
The mountains are high ... The
Cherokee ... may not love you ...
the beasts and the serpents of
the wilderness lurk in harm's way."
jRobbins

CHAPTER 13

THE NORTH GEORGIA MOUNTAINS

Hamlet had decided not to begin his long-awaited memoirs as far back as he could remember. He would start at Spring Place, where Samuel was born. Therefore, it was not to St. Augustine that Hamlet's memory now traveled, but to a mountaintop in Georgia.

1811. "I remember, Son, putting you in front of me in the saddle and riding far out into the North Georgia Mountains on Butterfly, our "legs" at that time. We were living in Spring Place and your mother had just passed. You were only two and it was early spring. I can still feel the fresh, warm breeze on our faces that morning. It's all very clear in my mind as I think back."

Hamlet spoke in a far-away voice in the slow motion of another time remembered. "All winter I had been tossing an idea around: that of leaving the land of the Cherokee. White Panther, my apprentice, had told me of a path through the white-faced Cumberland Mountains, which led to the Shawnee Indian nation—a sometime enemy of the Cherokee. He told me there were many Europeans who had settled there among the natives. I began to realize that where there were Europeans, there could be German settlements: communities where I might discover other Shucks.

"There was nothing in Spring Place to hold me. Your mother was gone and I had to face it. We needed to get on with our lives—get on with the search for our roots. Your mother and I had planned to make the search together. We knew that someday you would want to know the country of your origin as much as I did."

The Crone on the Mountain

This is the story he told, though not in his own words:

Upon reaching the summit of a high ridge, Butterfly—the same horse that had carried him from the mission three years earlier—halted when Hamlet pulled up on the reins. She was beautiful with her lustrous black mane and tail. Brother Hector had given him the best two-year-old mare at the mission. Soft black markings outlined her ears and nose, as well as the hair about her hooves. Her rich coat was as white as the snow on the distant peaks in high winter.

The mare had born a foal the year after Hamlet came to live at Spring Place and another one the next. The first of the offspring was a colt, which Hamlet named Hector after the master weaver who had given him the mare. Except for a brown star on his forehead, his white coat with its distinguishing black appointments was a replica of his mother's. The second foal was a filly, which Hamlet called Star. She was black from nose to tail with the same brown star on her forehead that marked her brother.

Both had been born of wild stallions that sometimes visited the grassy pastures where Butterfly and the other village horses grazed. The two animals were high-spirited like their wild sires; but Hamlet's gentle nurturing, along with Butterfly's docile disposition, had tamed Hector and Star into sterling, strong-hearted, yet genial horses. Either one would allow young Samuel to sit on a blanket on its back for a ride. Hamlet walked alongside Samuel, of course, around the spacious corral and fields behind their cabin. He hoped that one day he could return a steed to the brothers at the mission, yet doubted that he would ever get that way again.

However, on this beautiful morning, Hamlet's mind was not on his premier horses. He could see the majesty of the impenetrable-looking rock formations in the distance—a scene above Spring Place he had often looked upon—and his mind was restless. Taking in the tantalizing vista, he said, "Look, Son! See all those mountains and trees out there?"

Samuel, who was playing with Butterfly's lustrous black mane, looked down his father's arm, on past his pointed finger, and said "Yes" in a playful, happy singsong voice. Unimpressed with the view, the two-year-old looked back down at the silken strands in his hands—which, at that particular moment, were far more interesting to him than the misty wilderness. He twirled the long hair around his chubby little fingers, pulled it through his mouth until it was wet, and generally held onto it to feel secure in the saddle.

"Do you see all that haze and in those grandfather hills?" Hamlet asked the boy. "Looks like smoke, doesn't it?"

Again, Samuel looked toward the mountain range. "Yes, Papa. Smoke."

Hamlet marveled at the depth of understanding that his two-year-old son had incorporated into his vocabulary. They could actually have simple conversations. He hugged Samuel affectionately, climbed down from the horse, and lifted the boy to the ground. "How about some lunch?"

Samuel was always ready to eat. Reaching up, he scrambled toward the deerskin pouch that hung from the horn on the saddle. He knew it held their lunch because he had helped pack it that morning. Hamlet handed the lunch bag to Samuel and took the saddle off the horse. Butterfly walked away to graze in some fresh mountain grass.

Hamlet spread the saddle blanket on the ground and stopped for a moment to study it. It told a story. He had lived among the Seminoles and the Cherokees long enough to appreciate their art and beliefs. Sometimes he incorporated a shaman, whose tales told of the ancient ones who protected and guided the spirit world. However, the design woven into this blanket was a classic Indian theme: a spirit quest. This was a ritual of a young brave setting out on his own, without food or water, to seek his destiny through a vision into the spirit world of his Creator. A young boy would wait with outstretched arms for a vision to come to him—perhaps in the form of a human or animal. Sometimes, such a novitiate would later etch the vision on a smooth rock or on the wall of a cave. The etchings left down through thousands of years are petroglyphs.

The coverlet was a palette of color, made from the yarn of sheep wool and wild cotton—both of which he had dyed with native plants and minerals. Spun goat hair reinforced its corners—a technique he had learned from an imported Bedouin slave. The man was among those outcasts of society who had found refuge with the brothers at the St. Augustine mission.

Mother Earth chased Father Sky in the overall design. The top of the blanket featured streaks of orchid in an azure sky; the bottom held striations of vermilion and chestnut earth. Just above the ground, waves of sapphire and indigo water undulated. The bold happy sunburst in the body of the weaving varied from deep crimson, coral, jasmine, to gold—the living colors of the soul. An image in the center was the embodiment of the human spirit of the warrior with rayed headdress, whose aura fetched support from the spirit world.

Finally, woven into the sky and earth were images of Creator's works. Curly horned sheep from which man takes wool and food, the skeleton of a fish from the stream for nourishment and sewing tools, an owl to stand for the wisdom of the shaman, a deer to represent the reward of the hunter, and the hunter with arrow drawn. For thousands of years, men and women have considered these symbols while embarking on spirit quests. Mankind has searched for meaning in the universe; and men have dared to risk their lives on dangerous journeys to find wisdom. Hamlet's blanket summoned up a quest, upon which, he would embark in his own way.

Samuel tugged at his father's pant leg. "Who's that?" Hamlet looked down at Samuel and then to the spot where he was pointing. A woman, who appeared to be mourning, stood at the top corner of the pallet. Was she really there? He had seen this dim apparition of the weeping woman once before. She had hovered beside his loom—the loom at the mission on which he had woven his first intricate tapestry of a boy and girl dancing. It was the loom used to weave the blanket on which they now stood. Her lament then, as now, was, "Where are my children?"

He thought she was leaning forward to touch him, but suddenly realized that it was only Samuel, reaching up for his father. "Where she go, Papa? Why is she crying?"

Hamlet looked back and saw that the vision was gone. "I don't know, son. I don't know. There are things between sky and earth that we cannot understand. We must wait until the by and by where all the mysteries of life will be answered."

Young Samuel was pulling their lunch out of the tote: a skin of water and some "pasties." Hamlet plopped down beside the boy to give him a hand. "Here, let me help you with those, amigo."

After his wife, Anna, died, Hamlet learned to make meat and potato pastries from an English neighbor. The pastry was hard on the outside to protect the tasty contents on the inside. She had said that in the old country the pastie bread was so hard that one could drop it down a mineshaft and it would not break open. American pastie bread was not that hard because pioneers needed to make use of the entire food item, including the crust. English pastie bread was often too hard to eat. In the wilderness, where want was only a meal away, nothing was wasted.

BETWEEN TWO WORLDS

Hamlet and Samuel settled down to eat. Samuel dropped chunks of food on his shirt while he ate. Nothing wrong with his appetite! After they finished, both took a cool drink from the water skin and stretched out on the blanket to rest their lunches. Samuel was soon asleep, but Hamlet's mind was daydreaming. He looked out at the rolling peaks looming in the distance and said to himself, "I don't see how anybody—not even White Panther—could get through that wall of rock. It runs clear across the horizon, but he says he has passed through it many times.

"That Cherokee weaves more tales than fabric while he is at the loom," Hamlet said softly and smiled to himself. He thought of all the stories the Indian had told him about his birthplace, which was near a cave beyond the great plateau, which sprawled just over the mountain range before him now. Over the past three years, White Panther had painted stories of adventure and promise in the land to the north during their long days at the loom.

White Panther and Hamlet had lived together in the Indian's dwelling before Hamlet married Anna. The basket maker had talked Hamlet into showing him how to weave on a loom in return for a place to live. White Panther moved his things to a comfortable alcove near the back of his cave home and made a bed for Hamlet in the middle section near the fireplace. Hamlet assembled his looms just outside the cave opening in a huge, veranda-sort-of-a-man-made structure that jutted out from the mountainside.

The basket weaver had thatched its roof to keep out the rain. His veranda's sides consisted of maybe a dozen well-spaced cured saplings, on either side, latticed with grapevine to hold leafy vines for shade. The front of the structure was open so that he could watch the goings on in the village, as well as the evening sunsets in the west. His baskets lined one side of the back wall of the airy addition to protect them from the elements but ready to sell or trade. Straw mats covered most of the floor, upon which White Panther sat to weave his baskets.

White Panther had told Hamlet a legend about an immortal panther that guarded the great gap. He had told him, too, of the many deer hunting trips with his tribe that took them through the pass into a broad, remote and rugged plateau. As well, he had recounted Indian wars between the Cherokee and the Shawnee over those same high plateau hunting grounds in the gap near his birthplace.

Later, when he married Anna, Hamlet had built their own log cabin between the cave and the inn in Spring Place, but the two friends still made their living in the cave workplace.

Hamlet felt like he was between two worlds as he lay beside little Samuel on their spirit quest blanket.

"When did I become a man?" Hamlet asked himself.

That was when Hamlet first started thinking about continuing his search for his own beginnings.

The warm sun shining down on Hamlet and Samuel was soothing; and, at last, his eyes drooped into sleep. Sometimes, dreams show the way.

He dreamed of the day that he had left the mission on his own quest…

THE FERRY ACROSS THE ST. JOHN'S RIVER

Starting over, this time on his own, Hamlet followed the deerskin map north from St. Augustine until he came to the St. John's River ferry, which, he fancied, would carry him across the waterway to the rest of his life. It was noon and the ferry was on the opposite shore. He would have to wait for it to recross the wide span of water.

Three or four thatched dwellings stood along the shore. An old tribal man with very dark skin was scratching out a garden patch behind one of them, and he waved at Hamlet with a friendly smile.

"Seminole," Hamlet assured himself, when he saw that the man was wearing a red and yellow turban around his head and a blue sash about his waist.

Some children were peeking at him from behind a matt blind that served as a wall for one of the huts. When he waved at them, the shy faces instantly vanished in a fit of giggling. A pleasant warmth came over him when he saw the children playing, and he wished that he could have played with little friends as a child.

Inside another dwelling, a small group of women, who showed no sign of alarm at the visitor, was working on some sewing project—much like a quilting bee. They wore strand upon strand of beaded shell necklaces to adorn their brightly dyed, tiered blouses and skirts. Hamlet knew that if the women were very lucky, they owned a few strands of imported glass beads like the ones he would trade with the mico.

Maybe traveling alone would not be so bad, after all. He did not know the people who ran the ferry, but they were friendly.

Hamlet unhitched the horse and led it down to drink from shallows where cattails grew. He, too, cupped his hands and drank his fill. He was hungry but wanted to wait until he got the horse and carriage safely across the river before stopping to rest and eat. While he waited, he thought of getting out his maps but decided he would wait until nightfall to study them by the light of a glowing campfire. He let the mare graze for a few minutes and then hitched her back to the wagon. The better part of an hour passed, and the large log ferry was back.

The ferryman greeted him. When Hamlet spoke to him in the Muskogee language, the Seminole man seemed quite pleased to have the stranger and his load board the ferry. Before they started the crossing, the Indian went into one of the huts and returned with a skin of water and some corn cakes, which he shared with Hamlet on their crossing. Hamlet offered a vial of rich, red blood-root dye in return for the food and passage, which the ferryman accepted for payment with much delight.

Once across the river, Hamlet stopped only for a short while to eat some of the flavorful jerked pheasant and dried apples he had brought to eat while traveling. He gave the mare a few wild oats from a bag in the wagon. The trail would eventually lead him west to the place where the three rivers on the map met, where he would change the course of his route to due north.

Near nightfall, he stopped to make camp and settle in for his first night out on the long journey. He had seen no other people since the crossing and found the trail easy to follow. He also found the solitude in the semitropical flatland quite to his liking and comfort. Quiet by nature, he had always enjoyed the hours when he could be alone with his thoughts. The cries of the fabulous birds and the croaking and splashing of the thousands of frogs in the area provided a concert of nature's purest music.

Hamlet looked very much like a gypsy as he traveled west across the Surveyor's Trail, skirting a great swamp to get to the winding Suwannee River. His treasured map guided him along a low, wooded trail until he reached the confluence with the Alapaha and Withlacoochee rivers. The banks rolled up into ribbons of sand made smooth by frequent flooding where the three waterways met. In places, sandbars reached all the way to the rock corridor through which the waters ran. Large pine and oak trees grew on the limestone walls of the canyon. Hamlet forded the water where the sand had washed up a natural bridge under shallow water and quickly directed his horse inland to stay on course with the map.

By noon the next day, his water bags were empty. When he found a trail that descended to the river, Hamlet took it to restore his water supply. An odd color, the water was dark tannin and reeked with mineral gases. He noticed that the riverbed was hard, irregular, and most uninviting. It looked ominous;

and, when his horse would not drink, he filled only one water skin and then quickly left to escape the sickening air.

"Swift Weaver told me to stay away from the rivers for safety. I can see now that he meant that in many ways. This water smells like poison whether it is or not!"

When he came to a clear, narrow rivulet trickling through the limestone, he emptied the rank contents from his bag, rinsed it out, and filled it to the top with the better class of water. Both he and Butterfly, the beautiful mare Brother Hector had given him when he left St. Augustine, drank as much as they could from the pure mountain stream that originated above the rainbow of minerals in the strata below.

From there, he took the clearly sketched trail on Swift Weaver's map to stay between the two rivers flowing down from the north.

The tableland was dolloped with hillocks and the elevation crept steadily higher until natural patches of white escarpment, pushed up eons before from the ocean floor, peaked through virgin forestation.

Days passed.

The grades along the route were getting harder to overcome. He wondered whether Butterfly could continue to pull the heavy cart over the hilly terrain. One evening, after reaching the top of a particularly steep range of hills, he began to breathe more easily. Before him, the land sloped easily down to a river bottom. It was the westernmost of the two Georgia rivers on his map. A branch ran between the Withlacoochee and a very large, long lake that sparkled in the sunset. He knew it was the lake on Swift Weaver's map and could see the wide Flint River that reached right out of the top of it into Creek Indian territory.

As he sat there on the seat of the wagon looking down into the valley, he felt a sense of relief and let out a sigh, which he did not even know he was holding. Hamlet had started to fear a new challenge on his journey: the mountains. Tension had been steadily growing inside his young body. He had thought many times in the last few days that he still had time to go back down the same trail to Brother Hector and the mission haven. Now, he took heart when he remembered that the Flint would lead him to the mico in Coweta. He had completed his first leg of the trip safely and in good health; and, now, renewed courage sped him toward his goal.

"Uncle Mico"

The village was big. It was, in fact, not merely a village: it was a tribal town built around a great flat-topped mound of earth; and it bustled with the business of the Creek people. He had seen a few small Indian villages along the way and in the distance, but he had been afraid to approach any of them. Swift Weaver had told him that some Indians would not be friendly, that he should wait for the big village. Hamlet knew by the number of dwellings that he saw now, that this was Coweta, the village of his friend's Uncle Mico.

His Creek tongue had a limited vocabulary; but he hoped the alligator stick beside him on the cart would serve to show that he was coming in peace, that he was carrying the Creek totem to find favor. Actually, a large group of curious young braves and a sprinkling of small Indian boys had been following him up the Flint as he made his approach. He thought they seemed friendly, but fearing capture once he entered the settlement, his heart pounded at a furious pace in his chest. He drove slowly past rectangular dwellings built of grass and mud, and crowned with cypress bark shingles. He fairly crept as he entered the promenade around the base of the mound—open space that served as the center of industry and communal activity.

The one thing that really bothered him was the silence; the people had stopped what they doing to stare at the young man with a Spanish horse and cart as he passed by. A few times, he waved in friendship and held up the alligator stick for them to see; but none of them acknowledged his efforts. He decided that the best thing to do was to stop where he was and wait for someone to acknowledge him.

It could not have been more than a minute when he saw, whom he knew by the demeanor of the man, the chief of the Wind Creek clan: Uncle Mico. The handsome figure was descending the steps of the mound. Silence continued until the mico stopped at a spot within ten feet of the wagon and raised his hand to display the universal sign for peace. Hamlet stood up from his seat and hopped down to the ground with the walking-stick gift in his hand. The chief motioned for him to approach. The tension lifted the instant the mico saw the alligator staff and broke into a smile. He had accomplished the second leg on the map.

"Uncle Mico" had known instantly that the walking stick had come from one of his clan's members living in the southeast, because the carving represented Creeks from the deep south—alligator swamp country. The villagers gathered around Hamlet to welcome him. Because of the language barrier between them, conversation was scant; but if smiles could talk and actions could speak, it was a rich, meaningful occasion. Hamlet ate with them, slept in Uncle Mico's lodge, and traded with him the blue glass beads for buckskins. Sometime during the evening, Hamlet showed Swift Weaver's uncle his map with its Creek markings, which removed all doubt about which family member had sent the staff with Hamlet. 'Twas the son of his wife's sister, who studied at the mission in Florida.

Hamlet Shuck had rested for a day in the arms of the Wind Creek clan and was anxious and ready for the final trek to Spring Place in the North Georgia Mountains.

Spring Place

White Panther was the first person Hamlet met upon entering Spring Place. While riding into the edge of the settlement, Hamlet saw the basket maker, who was weaving a sweet grass basket outside his rock-cave house. The Indian greeted him warmly, shook hands, and directed him to the inn, where he could find food and lodging. White Panther was soon to become his apprentice and constant friend.

Hamlet found Spring Place to be a community of friendly people. A French trapper named Parker Louis had settled there in the late 1700s. He had built a pretty little two-room cabin and worked out of it: first to trap and then to host other trappers on their way to and from the eastern fur market. Later, Parker had taken a wife—the daughter of a fellow trapper from New York and his Cherokee wife. His new wife's name was Aurora; but by the time Hamlet arrived in Spring Place, she was known as the Widow Louis.

The original Louis cabin now served as the dining and sitting room of the inn. Louis had enlarged their home when their child, Anna, was born. He had built a second story onto the dwelling, which held both a sleeping loft for boarders and private rooms for his own family. In addition, he added a borning room and a summer kitchen to accommodate the needs of his growing family.

The Louis Inn, from the beginning, had been the center of activity. First, the trappers had come to know of his cabin and hospitality in the old abandoned Cherokee winter camp, where the Moravians had tried to start a mission, but failed. Then, Louis began to greet pioneers on their migration north or west and served as a message dispatcher when he could. Soon other white families had found the old camp as good a place to settle as any, and Spring Place was born. When Louis died from a bout of pneumonia four years back, Anna was twelve. It seemed practical, for survival, for Aurora to continue to maintain the Louis Inn. She and Anna together made a go of the business and both became post dispatchers.

His first night there, Hamlet was glad for the only bed he had felt since he left the mission. He had not realized how tired he was. The excitement in the new freedom he had gained had kept him on a fast pace north. He planned to stay on at the hospitable refuge for a couple of days to sleep in the loft and take his meals at the table spread for him and two other visitors to the village. Trappers, the men were laying over for provisions and a few days' rest before making the final leg of their due-east voyage, down the river to Savannah. Once there, the luxurious furs were shipped abroad and brought good money. Known for their heartiness and brawn, the trappers, he learned, made a prosperous living on the American frontier. The village people always looked forward to the tales of the wilderness, which the two men brought with them.

To his disappointment, Hamlet found that the German Moravians were gone. He decided to spend a whole week in Spring Place to plan out his next move in his search for a German community. During that week, Anna, a 16-year-old beauty, captured his heart.

*   *   *

Samuel kissed Hamlet awake....

CHAPTER 14

HAMLET'S QUEST

"The journey north is hard," White Panther, brow furrowed with concern, counseled Hamlet that evening. "Many rivers run against you. The mountains are high to block your way. The Cherokee braves may not love you like White Panther, and the beasts and the serpents of the wilderness lurk in harm's way."

"You, White Panther, are a Cherokee and you are my friend. The Seminoles were also my friends in St. Augustine. I do not fear the Native American; we are all men.

"I have traveled against the water since I left the mission and my horse doesn't care which way the water flows. He walks the trails beside it.

"I have faced wild stags in the wood and climbed some high hills. I do not fear the road. I have made many journeys since my childhood."

White Panther looked deep into Hamlet's eyes. "This journey is not the same. Some of the Cherokee know of you, but..."

"My heart," Hamlet interrupted, his eyes meeting those of the Indian, "says I must go. I will take my son, and I will go."

White Panther paused only a moment before finishing his sentence: "...the Shawnee do not know you!"

They stood silently then, searching each other's faces. "My friend...," White Panther again started to argue, but then stopped talking when he saw that Hamlet's expression had deepened with resolve. White Panther felt his face redden, his anger rise. He wanted to grab Hamlet and throw him to the ground to make him listen; but then, in the blink of an eye, he looked away—toward the foreboding blue mountains through which he had tried to warn his friend not to travel. Hamlet did not miss the Indian's growing frustration and quickly let his eyes fall to the ground; his breath escaped in a deep sigh. He looked up, first toward White Panther and then at the forbidding vista he planned to challenge. After a few moments, he turned back toward White Panther. One tear, two, fell from either eye of the defeated, sad-faced Indian. White Panther averted his face to brush tears away, and momentarily faced Hamlet. His face was a cross between defeat and understanding.

"I was wrong, my friend," he said to Hamlet, who had a restless, painful look about him. "You are right to want to find your people. The quest you are on is your life's force; it keeps you going. You cannot deny your heart, if you are to live.

Hamlet's gratitude began to shine through misty eyes, as he listened.

White Panther continued. "If you must go, I will take you to the end of the land of the Cherokee. Beyond there, the Shawnee live restlessly near the white settlers. I do not wish to cross into their territory. I will visit the place where I was born near the ancestral cave at the great gap before returning home. Now, with you gone, I will be both the best weaver of baskets and of blankets."

"I would like that, brother," Hamlet said with a wink.

WHITE PANTHER'S SECRET PLACE

A troubled White Panther walked out alone under a star-filled sky toward his favorite spot, a grassy hillside that overlooked the village. He felt close to Creator there among the lush green ferns and mountain laurel that grew beneath spreading hackberry trees and, often, went there to sort out his cares. He was not a young man, nor was he old. Once married, his wife had died when the secluded valley was little more than a small Cherokee winter encampment. No children had been born to their home and hearth.

He had buried her that winter in a tiny cave nearby, which he sealed off permanently with rocks and red clay. White Panther grieved for his young wife and withdrew to his cave and his work. Seasons came and went but he never took another wife. He no longer looked forward to the summer hunts with the members of his tribe and began staying behind to maintain the camp. An artist, he took on the task of weaving the intricate designs of his heart and heritage into mats and baskets for storage. Harvesting the many and colorful grasses that grew there in summer, he supplied the whole tribe, upon their return in late fall, with beautiful new baskets and floor coverings for the coming year.

Then, pioneers began to settle in the region. Fewer members of the Cherokee tribe returned to the age-old winter grounds each year. Many came back only long enough to trade food for baskets from White Panther, and then retreated into the surrounding forests and hills to avoid exposure to the whites. His Cherokee brothers were not surprised when White Panther decided to remain in the valley and to live among the white settlers, who named the growing community, Spring Place.

White Panther's friendly disposition and his fine baskets soon won the hearts of all who came to the village. However, knowing Hamlet was the best thing that had happened to him since his mate passed. It was time now for White Panther to become a scout, once more, to lead Hamlet and Samuel through the wilderness. One day, he would return to his valley to live out his years and rest beside the lovely Indian maiden who was his truest joy in life.

On Leaving Spring Place

That same night, Hamlet lay by the fireplace on a woven grass mat, propped up on one side with his arm under his head. Young Samuel lay curled up against his belly. The nights were still chilly even though spring had arrived; he watched the low flames leap up and then die before reaching the chimney hole. Glancing now and again through the window, which he always left slightly ajar to vent the cabin, he could see smoke rising from the other dwellings down along the shimmering lake under a full moon.

Hamlet's mind swam in circles. In the darkness, he thought about life there with Anna, his departed wife, only to think back, even farther, to his bizarre childhood aboard the pirate ship, his seven-year apprenticeship at the mission, and his flight into the wilderness to search for some clue to his long-lost beginnings. Then, his thoughts would flip flop and he would try to imagine what lay ahead, what the future would bring. Would he ever find his people? Hope sprang in his chest when he thought about the possibility. He had a gnawing feeling that somehow, sometime in his life, fate would lead him to the answer he had sought since childhood.

He knew that when he left Spring Place, some of his heart would stay behind, buried in the rock and clay grave that held Anna. In a way, she would not be left behind, for part of her would go with him—little Samuel. Samuel was Anna in so many ways—his curly strawberry blond hair, his ready smile and his natural curiosity about anything new. A bit timid at the onset of a new discovery, he soon fully immersed himself into the adventure of learning everything he could about the thing. Samuel was Hamlet, too. An uncommonly strong affinity for his father had been evident from the time the baby was born. His father was his hero, whom he mimicked at every turn. The boy was a constant source of joy for Hamlet. He did everything he could to let his son know that he was his father and that he could depend on him. As well, Hamlet constantly reminded Samuel that Anna was his mother and that she was still the heart of their home.

This particular night, Hamlet was on the edge of discovery and he knew it. It was well after midnight before sleep came. Finality had fallen peacefully over him as another chapter of his life closed behind him.

Early next morning, Hamlet stoked up the fire, added a little wood, unbolted the cabin door, and stepped out into another promising morning. There was a new sparkle in his eye as he stretched, raising his arms and fingers toward the sky as though he were pulling life-giving strength from it. He looked back inside the cabin and across the room at Samuel, still sleeping. One-quarter Cherokee, the child's complexion was a shade darker than Hamlet's. However, he had his father's fair hair, which lay in tousled blond ringlets on the pillow.

Satisfied that Samuel was still asleep, Hamlet walked with a skip in his step down the path to the smoke house where he cut a slab of meat off a ham hanging along with some other smoked game and fish.

Before leaving the smoke house, he looked around to take mental stock of what he might want to take with them when they left. As usual, on the heels of winter, there was not much left.

Hamlet loved a good breakfast. It was one meal he did not mind fixing. The smell of smoked meat, frying in a pan, and fresh coffee brewing somehow civilized the wilderness, whether he was in his own cabin or out on a forest trail.

Sitting before the fireplace on a three-legged stool, Hamlet took down the fry pan and ladled in a spoonful of bear fat. Skillfully trimming off the seasoned edges of the meat, he dropped it in to sizzle in the hot grease. The aroma of ham and hickory soon filled the air. Adding water to a cupful of cornmeal, he dropped several spoons of the mixture around the edges of the meat to cook.

The combined aroma of the brewing coffee and the hickory-smoked ham crawling through the open window was too much for White Panther to resist. Before the meal was on the table, Hamlet's Indian companion strolled into the cabin—just as Hamlet had hoped he would. The solemn conversation between the two men the night before was still heavy on his mind.

"You need somebody to help you eat that?" White Panther asked, smiling.

"I thought I might have company this morning. I was just sitting down." He motioned White Panther to join him.

By then, a sleepy little curly-head was sitting up in the middle of the bed, rubbing the sleep out of his eyes. When he saw that White Panther was there, his face lit up and he bounced out of the covers and crossed the floor to the Indian's lap. Samuel loved White Panther almost as much as his own father, because he spent most of his waking hours playing around the weaver's house, where White Panther lived and worked with his father. The man doted on Samuel like the son he never had.

White Panther did not have the first mouth of food down before he felt the sensation of warmth soaking through his buckskin trousers. He jumped up and ran to the door, holding the boy out in front of him for the stream to run out onto the ground. Hamlet was laughing at the perturbed look of his friend. "Don't look at me!" he said. You picked him up!"

The water-soaked diaper slipped off Samuel and fell to the ground. "I'm cold!" Samuel fussed and scrambled to get down and back into the warm cabin. Hamlet wrapped him in a blanket and put him in his own chair to eat the diced meat and spoon bread that he had fixed for him.

Neither of the two men mentioned the previous day's events while they were eating. But, later, when they were walking toward the weaving room, Samuel galloping along on his carved wooden stick horse, White Panther was first to broach the subject. "So, have you changed your mind or are you still bound to go?"

"What do you think?"

"That's what I thought,"

The two walked on in silence for what seemed ages to Hamlet. He hoped White Panther had not changed his mind about going with him.

His fears vanished when White Panther went on to ask, "Well, when do we leave?"

Hamlet smiled and let out a long breath. "How long do you think it'll take us to get ready?"

That depends on what all you intend to take. Are you taking the furniture in the cabin?"

"No," Hamlet said. "Anything of real value belongs to Aurora, anyway. Annie and I went to housekeeping on her extra furniture. We never really had a chance to get much on our own.

"Seems like we just got settled in when the baby came and in a little while, she was gone." Hamlet's voice faltered and his eyes held a dull ache.

Regaining a little composure, he said, "I always wondered whether Aurora blamed me for Annie's death."

"Why?" White Panther asked. "Small pox can take anybody—and besides, nobody is better at treating sickness than an Indian woman. Aurora is half Cherokee! She did all she knew to save her daughter. Didn't she send you and Samuel away to stay with me to protect you? Didn't she stay with her Anna day and night?"

"I know," Hamlet said, "but before I came here, Anna was alive and healthy. After I came, she died. The Cherokee look to the Spirit Father for the answers to many things. Perhaps she blames me. Sometimes, I, myself, feel like a wicked spell rides the dust at my heels!"

"Think no such thing! I am Cherokee. Aurora is Cherokee. I know the Cherokee. Aurora is glad you gave Anna a son and herself a grandson before her daughter died. Many times she has said this."

"She may not be so glad now," Hamlet said, "now that I am taking her grandson away."

White Panther thought for a moment, "In that, my friend, you may be right."

Quickly, Hamlet's face perked up. "I could ask her to come with us!"

"Ask!" White Panther said. "But she will not leave. Her parents, her husband, and her daughter are all buried here in this place, where her blood runs deep."

"I know that," Hamlet said, softly. "But when I tell her we're going, I will ask her anyway."

"Then, what will you do with the looms and the horses?" White Panther inquired next.

"The horses go!" Hamlet said. "They are all that I really own of value. I could not leave them behind. Anyway, Star and Hector remind me that life goes on. They are Butterfly's family and they should be together."

White Panther shook his head, "Hamlet, I don't always know what you mean. They are animals. You think they are people. I agree you should take them—they are best horses I have seen."

Hamlet was not really listening to his friend. His mind was speeding ahead. "It will be different than when I traveled before. I will take only the looms I came with, the rest are yours. You helped build them—you should keep them for your return."

White Panther looked pleased; but, before he could say anything, Hamlet finished the thought he had really started out to express: "This time will be different, because of Samuel. It has been a year since his mother passed, and you have gotten by—with Aurora's help. It won't be so easy, traveling with a child."

Breakfast finished, Hamlet took up the plates and placed them in soapy water to let them soak. After dressing Samuel, he and White Panther went to the workshop to finish their talk.

Samuel rode his wooden stallion, Little Star, all the way there. Once inside, he continued to ride all around the cave and the rock veranda. White Panther had woven a horse's head from broom grass, complete with buckeye eyes and corn shuck ears, and attached to it to a length of cedar sapling with wet leather bands. When the bands dried, the two pieces fit tightly. He pulled another leather thong through a hole bored in the sapling for Samuel to hold as he rode on imaginary hunting trips. Sometimes he led the horse as though there was a rider on it—like his father often led Star with Samuel sitting on her.

"Maybe you should ask Aurora," White Panther said.

"Ask her what?" Hamlet asked, obviously lost in his son's game of pretend.

"What to take!" White Panther said. "She'll know what a growing-up boy needs."

"You're right," Hamlet agreed. "A woman, only, knows what a growing-up boy needs."

"And what will you take?" Hamlet asked White Panther.

"Only my pony and blanket;" he answered and then quickly added, "trail cakes and the medicine pouch, too."

Aurora did not cry when Hamlet told her about his plan to leave Spring Place. She had seen it coming since the day he first ate at her boarding house table, but had hoped it would not come too soon. She could judge a person's needs from having seen so many people come and go through her doors. Hamlet was a man with a mission. She read it in his eyes, heard it in his stories; and had expected it since Anna's death.

Cradling her grandson in her arms, Aurora set her face so that she would not cry. "No. This is your destiny and the destiny of my grandson. My home is here, where I plan someday to rest forever beside my husband and child.

"I have always known you would have to go someday. I thought you would take my Anna with you in the search for your people. However, in the end, you are leaving her here, with me. Instead, you are taking the child of her spirit— my grandson."

Hamlet felt that his heart would break as the tears welled up once again in his eyes—this time spilling over. "Oh! Aurora. How can I take him from you? In the year passing, you have been both mother and grandmother."

Aurora reached out a comforting hand to Hamlet. "Why do you cry, my son? It is a good thing you do now. My grandson will know who his mother's people were; but, if you do not try, he will never know who his father's father was.

"Hamlet, my life is fulfilled now that I know I have a grandson to carry it on; but his life and your life will never be whole unless you find the way to your father's hearth.

"It'll be hard to see you both go—for I fear that I'll never see you again. But it would be harder, in the end, if you do not go; because someday Samuel will need the same thing in his life that you do—to know who he is."

Her gentle smile and touch soothed Hamlet's countenance and he enveloped this mother of mothers and his son in his arms. His face against Aurora's, at last he felt the warm tear coursing its way between her face and his to fall to the wooden floor beneath them.

Aurora advised Hamlet to trade his small mission cart for her own sturdier canvas-covered wagon. It would take both Butterfly and Star to pull the much heavier wagon. Tethered behind, Hector followed. The wagon would afford enough sleeping space for Hamlet, Samuel, and even White Panther in inclement weather.

In less than a week, Hamlet Shuck and his party left Spring Place for a new wilderness beyond the Smoky Mountains—the Cumberland Plateau.

"It'll take the wisdom of a shaman
to bring her back..."

Chapter 15

The Darkest Hour

Hamlet and Samuel had lived a long time since their North Georgia mountain days. They never made it back to Samuel's maternal grandmother, Aurora; however, both now believed they knew the truth, through the silver pendants, about the Shuck family from which they had descended. The proof of it, Hamlet thought, lay across a wide ocean in the German Schwarzwald. Samuel was satisfied with knowing he was of German descent—genealogy meant little to him; however, his father was far from the end of his journey. The absolute proof, indeed, the whole truth, would have to wait for a while longer...

Out in the damp, cold woods, the spirit of Frau Gertrude von Shuck attended her daughter. Sparrow nestled her head in her mother's lap while Frau Shuck lovingly cradled her child's face and stroked her long silver hair.

"Does it hurt very much, my dear?" Gertrude asked.

"Not so very much. I just can't wake up."

"I know, child. You're unconscious."

"You're my mother, aren't you?"

"I am, indeed. I have been looking for you for a very long time. We're a long way from home, you know."

"Home?"

"Germany. The Black Forest. That's where you and your twin brother were born."

"So...he *is* my brother then. Were we really kidnapped?"

"So it seems." Gertrude kissed Sparrow's forehead. "It's taken all these years of searching to find you both."

The two went silent as they enjoyed the halcyon of the moment of sweet reunion. After a while, Frau Gertrude gently laid her daughter's head back into the fragrant pine needles on the forest floor and took a few steps into the edge of the dark woods. "I can rest in peace now," she said. "I must be going."

"Are you coming back?" Sparrow asked.

"No, child. I'll wait for you on the other side," the fading spirit said. "Or, did you think you would come with me now?"

"Well," Sparrow said. "I don't know for sure. Am I still alive? I feel so good with you."

"For now, yes; you are still breathing the air of the green woods around you. If this is your time to cross over, we will soon be together; if it is not, I'll watch over you until you come." The spirit was gone.

"Holy smoke! There she is!" the nix, Katie, barked and broke into a run. "She's hurt! And Brother Peacock is with her!"

The little black dog tried to lick Sparrow awake to no avail—and, she tasted blood. Suddenly it occurred to her that the peacock should have gone for help.

"What in the devil is wrong with you? Why are you just lying there?"

The bird was stiff, cold, and altogether peeved at the dog's remarks. Hadn't he stopped the bleeding? Brother Peacock blurted out a quick defensive squawk.

"Oh, never mind!" Katie barked. "I'm going to get Shane!" She leaped past the peacock and ran back toward the cabin.

Black Hawk's amazing aerial vision did not let him down. The nix was moving—no, flying—down below. It was clear she was retreating straight back down her assigned search route. "Ha! She knows something. She is going back to Watcher in the sycamore! I'm right behind her!"

While the middle wood was abuzz with activity—the nix and the black crow rushing on one direction and Mack and Shane about to meet them from the opposite direction—the brownie and the banshee encountered each other at the top of the woods where east path met west. They both saw the fallen Sparrow at once.

"Oh, no," Keen lamented. "No. Not my Sparrow." The banshee was on the verge of keening when she caught herself. She was trying to remember something; it was about facing fear: facing fear and the propensity of the human spirit to live on forever. The banshee, instead of keening, which was the most expected behavior of her genus, went sober.

"Look!" Pitt said. "The eyes of the peacock's plumes cover Miss Sparrow's forehead. Is she dead?" The two sprites hurried to her side and saw the dark pool of blood on the ground. Carefully, the brownie slid his small hands under the bird's remedy to stop the bleeding—the stack of plumes, eye upon eye. The banshee lit on Sparrow's wrist to try to find any sign of a pulse. It was weak, yet discernible.

Pitt suddenly noticed that Keen was not moaning and crying over Sparrow. "Here?" he said, to use a typical English expression. "What's this? No keening?"

"Now is the time to be strong," she answered. "She's alive."

Kate saw Mack and Shane's twinkling gourd lantern before she heard them. Her heart quickened as their familiar voices became audible and she picked up her pace at the welcomed sound. Help was at hand.

One of the advantages of being a dog, as well as a fairy, was that one could hear Kate's bark long before that of a human voice or a nix. Shane and Mack picked up their pace the instant they heard the wee bark. There was no question that Katie would lead them to Grandmother Sparrow.

"Hurry!" Shane said. "She has found her!"

The dog, her master, Mack, and his new father-in-law sped down the trail and quickly reached the spot where Sparrow lay alongside her constant companion, the peacock.

The ghastly scene before them was hard. "Mother!" Shane cried and threw himself to the ground beside her.

Dr. Mack Riley was going to be tested—really tested—for the first time since he became a licensed doctor. For a moment, he panicked; this was, after all, his new wife's grandmother. After a few frozen moments, he took control of the one thing he hoped he would not have to face—that Sparrow had come to harm. He was, after all, the only doctor in the Riley Mill community.

"Please, Shane," he said as he pulled him away from his mother. "Let me see whether she has a pulse."

"Yes; barely."

With that, he moved Brother Peacock out of the way and gently took Sparrow into his arms and started back through the woods for the cabin. All the while, with each step, he tried to think what he would do for her. "It'll take the wisdom of a shaman to bring her back," he thought to himself and prayed for guidance from his own great Healer.

Meanwhile, all the fairies had gathered, again, in the Enchanted Tree with Watcher and Chelsea. As planned, the ground squirrel had a repast of tea and cakes ready for the exhausted searchers.

The two men made haste and in only minutes were back at the cabin with poor Sparrow. A shocked Keren-happuck and Rose were quick to throw back the covers on the bed in the small sleeping room off the main living area. Rose brought a pitcher of warm water she had filled from the fireplace kettle and poured it in its matching bowl at the washstand. Keren-happuck began to wash the caked blood from her unconscious grandmother's face, while Rose brought a down quilt from the bureau to place on the ashen Sparrow. Doctor Mack quickly asked his friend, Jon, to retrieve the medical bag from his carriage.

The young physician inspected the wound left by Black Hawk's arrow to find that it had stopped bleeding but that swelling had set in. It was a deep cut, the cause of which eluded him. "I wonder what caused that gash," he said. "What on earth could have done that?"

To reduce the swelling, Mack cleaned the area with witch hazel from a vial in his bag. To keep the fresh wound from starting to bleed again, he covered it with nettle leaves taken from a pouch in his bag. With another vial, he saturated a clean bandage to make a poultice of nettle tea for its iron and Vitamin C properties.

Next, he listened to Sparrow's chest with his stethoscope to find that the trauma of lying in the damp woods and the loss of blood had left her near death. "Rose?" he asked. "Do you have any willow bark to make tea? She is starting a fever and she'll need it."

"Yes, Mack," she said. "Should I make some lemon balm tea to help sweat it out?"

"That wouldn't be a bad idea," he agreed. "I just hope we can get both of them down her."

Jon Clay woke up and began to fuss. Of course, Hamlet left off storytelling when Shane and Mack rushed in with his sister and retreated to an out-of-the-way corner. Jesse tried to hush the child, but he wanted his bed.

"Is there anything we can do?" Abigail asked from the bedroom door.

Doctor Mack spoke. "You all should go. All we can do now is wait."

"Yes," Rose said. "You'd better get those babies home. We'll let you know if there's any news."

The Shuck family left the cabin with heavy hearts. Their worse fears had come to fruition. Before he went to the carriage, Grandfather Hamlet looked into the room at his twin sister. She looked quite different now from the mysterious woman who had been so agitated at his arrival just the night before—so small, so pale; but, considering her grave condition, she had an extraordinarily peaceful countenance upon her face.

"I've seen this before," he spoke softly, "in the faces of those who have come to terms with their lives. It is a good thing. If she passes, I will be sorry at not having known her."

For the next few hours, Sparrow's condition gradually worsened. Her temperature increased and the swelling about her head became more prominent. "I wish I had some quinine," Doctor Mack lamented. "She needs quinine if we are to have any chance of saving her."

Keren-happuck suddenly remembered that her grandmother used the bark from dogwood trees to make a quinine substitute. She quietly slipped out of the room and out to Sparrow's loft to see whether she could find some. The only thing was that she was not sure what it looked like. "Oh, dear!" she cried. "I wish I had paid more attention to what all these gatherings are."

"I know," a banshee voice said.

Keren looked around and saw that the entire search party of fairies and enchanted animals had joined her in the loft. They stood huddled together around the banshee, Keen, Sparrow's lifelong guardian; and all were fully transfigured into visible entities. "Keen! Pitt!" she gasped. "Hello, everyone! What are you all doing here?"

"We have come to try to help Miss Sparrow," Watcher volunteered before Keen could answer. "What can we do?"

"Well, I'm looking for dogwood bark for Grandmother. Mack says he needs quinine to treat her and I know that she uses dogwood bark as a substitute for it."

Keen stepped a little forward and crossed her arms in front of her. "I said, Watcher, that I know!"

Keren-happuck was quick to ask, "Which one is it, Keen?"

"That's it," the banshee pointed and quickly flew up to the shelves of herbs and roots to show Keren.

"Thank you, Keen," the young woman said gratefully and took a few pieces in her hand and ran down the stairs and back into the house.

"Mack!" she said. "Here! This is what Grandmother uses in place of quinine!"

"Dogwood bark?" he questioned her. "I've read about Indians using this. Hmm. I guess we could try it."

Keren marveled that her husband knew what kind of bark it was. "I'll have Mother make a strong tea from it."

While the decoction simmered, Dr. Mack resumed his vigil at Sparrow's side. "It would be good," he told Shane, "for the rest of you to get some rest. All

we can do now is wait. I will take the first watch. Don't worry, I'll let you know
if there's a change."

Shane agreed and laid comforters before the fireplace for a place for the
family to try to get some sleep. "Come, daughter; come Rose. Lay yourselves
down beside me and rest."

Helplessly, Mack watched Grandmother Sparrow sink into a darker and
deeper coma. He tried to pour as much of the homemade quinine tea between
her lips as possible, but very little of it went down. Weary, he closed his eyes
and rested his head against the back of the rocking chair in which he sat. Near
dawn, he awakened to find that the grand old Irish widow had slipped away
during the night. She had awakened from a dream called life.

CHAPTER 16

OLD DRUID OF THE BLACK FOREST

Hamlet stood in the grass beside the hand-hewn oak and pine box in which his sister lay under a mountain of wildflowers. He had lived half a century, was fifty years old, and had just found the only relative he had ever known—besides, of course, his own son and his family. Yes, he found her only to lose her to an accident in the not-quite-tamed Indiana wilderness. The preacher from the Franklin Presbyterian Church stood ready to perform the graveside rites before the large group of mill community neighbors who were still arriving to pay last respects. The burying ground was in the shadow of the three-story Riley's Mill landmark, with its giant turning wheel, which was to witness more than a hundred such occasions in the years to come.

Grandfather Shuck watched as friends walked from carriage to graveside across the lush green grass in the shade of a grove of walnut trees. He almost felt like a stranger even though he had once lived on the nearby homestead that Samuel, his son, now farmed. He saw Keren-happuck slip her fingers into her father's large, strong hands. Both wept silently, trying not to show their tears. Hamlet had mixed emotions: he felt no sense of great loss of a loved one, but he did feel a sense of regret that he had not gotten to know the tall, tanned woman of the woods who was his twin. From the number of mourners who had come out, he allowed to himself that she must have been a very special person. He would never really know.

As the last of the visitors arrived, Shane took up the Fiddle O'Shea and began to play the ancient dirge of farewell, "Going Home." The violin's pure and poignant musical sounds rose and fell in the stillness of a Sugar Creek afternoon. Chills coursed through Hamlet's body, as well as through all present, and hardly a breath escaped that was not essential. The old violin spoke the loss that Shane was feeling behind closed, soulful eyes.

A prayer, a short benediction, and "Shall We Gather at the River" over, the subdued assembly quietly spoke words of comfort to Keren-happuck and Shane as they filed past and went home. Only a few acknowledged that Hamlet had lost a sister, only a few knew.

Down in the far corner of the fencerow behind the cemetery, a group of solemn onlookers—Kate, Pitt, Keen and Watcher—had gathered to watch the ceremony and burial. The American Spirits knew that their roles would all change now that Sparrow had joined the ages.

When the last of the people had gone home, the fairies went to tend the crushed grass and errant pieces of earth around Sparrow's plot. That chore done, they tidied the petals of the flowers into perfect shapes to receive the dew from another of nature's caretakers—the living gray mantle that crept on mist tendrils all through the night to settle the dust of the day.

The three fairies trudged through blades of grass, past giant sugar maples, and down the path to the old Sycamore while Watcher circled above. They would talk that night of many things but most of all, of change.

The nix had zoned in on Grandfather Hamlet's thoughts over the last few hours; indeed, had awakened to the realization that the old druid of the ancestral quest would resume his search now. After all, his watch fob had contained the secret: his parents were from the Black Forest of Germany; he had a twin sister, Grandmother Sparrow; and his real name was Clovis and her name was Claire. In the fairy ring that night, Katrina spread her glimmering wings while transforming into a fully formed nix. The enchanted forest creatures and the fairies grew quiet as the sprite stood before them.

"He's bound for Germany, you know."

"Who?" Keen asked regarding the curious statement.

"Grandfather Shuck. Oh! He doesn't know it yet but it will be soon."

"And you'll be going with him then?" Pitt said more than asked.

"Yes. Of course. He will need guidance if he is ever to find his birthplace. I do not have to tell you that fairies are the embodiment of singular fates.

"I'll be glad, in a way, to return to the place of my own origin. I have not seen the nixies of the Schwarzwald for half a century. I should think that I would enjoy that very much."

"But you can't leave," Keen lamented. "What of the child, John Clay? By rights, you really are the Shuck's home fairy, are you not? And the little one will need a spirit guide very soon."

"I know," Katrina sighed. "He's already as bright as sun on quartz. I will have to fly my wings off with that one! However, I have mixed allegiances between the Shucks and the Rileys. I feel responsible for both families.

"But, Hamlet faces more than he can imagine."

"Oh?" Pitt raised his eyebrows.

"Well, I mean, he will find his old home with his mother's tombstone in the yard; but he will not, of course, find his father's stone."

"Oh, dear," the brownie said. "I remember now. Herr Shuck passed on in America just after he came across from the old country. He never knew that his son, Hamlet, even lived in America, did he?"

"Sadly, no," the nix said, as she thought back to that time. "He was going to start over; but I think he would have, at least, kept an eye out for his twins, kidnapped as they were from their beds when they were two."

"So, how did the old man die?" Pitt went on, with all the curiosity of his genre of the Faire.

"It was the ship—a bad crossing. Day after day, it rained until there wasn't a dry thread on the passengers. I nearly died of the damp, myself. I was miserable! By the time we landed on American soil, Herr Shuck, along with a dozen other passengers, was suffering just awful from congestion. The shipmates delivered them to an infirmary. Most died—among them, Herr Shuck."

"Where was he buried?" Pitt asked.

"A public burial ground in Charles Town in the Carolinas. He actually had quite a stash of gold coin in his sea trunk. I never did know what became of that. I suppose someone stole it. Between the ship's crew, the quacks running the sick clinic, and the undertaker, it just disappeared, trunk and all!"

"And, you, lass?" the brownie asked with genuine concern for the nix. "What became of you during all this?"

"I was in a right state for a while! I didn't know what to do. The old man was dead—and his wife, too; indeed, the twins, too, for all I knew."

"You must have been very confused, dear," Keen joined the conversation now. "I'm having some of the same feelings after losing Miss Sparrow."

"Yes," Pitt interjected. "But you still have plenty of family to care for, Keen."

"I guess it isn't the same," the banshee conceded." So what did you do, Kate?"

"I did what Herr Shuck would have done. It was all I could think of: I set off to see America and eventually found the Rileys who were living in Kentucky at the time.

"You know the rest...Schoolmaster Riley and the snow storm..."

Watcher had been listening to the fairies and now joined in. "Let's keep our eye on the situation at hand.

"I'm a little confused about why you feel such a strong responsibility toward Hamlet. He is grown and in his September years. "Why does he need you so much, Katrina?"

"Grandfather Hamlet," she answered, "has searched so long that I fear he will not be satisfied with just knowing who he is. He'll be disappointed with not finding his father's place of rest in Germany."

"Hmm," Pitt brooded. "I see what you mean. Hamlet can be as tenacious as a tick."

"Ten...what?" Keen exclaimed. "My gosh, Pitt. Speak English!"

"It *is* English, Keen! You know, tenacious—sticking to a task until you get it figured out!"

Keen gave the brownie a cool look. "Why don't you try to speak both the old Irish language and modern English, too? It's hard to remember every word! How many languages do you know? Never mind," she said icily, "I know. You can only speak one. Pity."

The wise Watcher intervened from his perch. "I say. This is no time for rivalry between your two countries. Our Kate has a real dilemma on her hands."

"Sorry, Kate," the two said at once and grew quiet again.

After a few pensive moments, Katrina went on. "Oh, well. Not to worry. I must look at this as an opportunity. I'm sure I will think of something to make his quest more easily passing.

"Besides, I'm not the only one here, you know, that faces an adjustment. You shall mourn Miss Sparrow, Keen. You have been together so long."

"True," the banshee agreed. "True. Nevertheless, I know that Miss Sparrow is not gone. Her spirit will fill these woods as long as Shane or any of his descendants inhabit the land. She will live in them—the Clan O'Shea—long after the memory of her is lost to the ages. Some day, perhaps far in the future, a child will be born with Sparrow's "old soul" staring out of "familiar striated green eyes," and she will be there. Another child may have an uncommon affinity for herbal tea—a genetic memory from her.

"No, Katrina. She lives on quite fully in the lives of Shane and Kerenhappuck and her special child, Elizabeth."

"What!" Pitt said, his peaked ears perking up. "Elizabeth? A new baby? Do you know something we don't?"

"Indeed?" Watcher hooted in a tone of curiosity.

"Oh, don't worry," Keen assured them. "Not for a while. I shouldn't have said anything about it at all. It's just a spark in the plan for this clan that will burst forth one day. I can tell you this: they will call the child Lizzy."

"Very good, Keen." Pitt patted the banshee's knee. "Very good. You never cease to amaze me. One moment, you don't even know a simple English word like tenacious and the next you seem to be in charge of the whole of knowledge."

Keen blushed at both the compliment and the brownie's bold pat on her bare knees. She quickly pulled her wispy gossamer gown down to her ankles.

Pitt, then, started to wonder whether his own life would change with the death of Grandmother Sparrow, not to mention the marriage of Keren-happuck. "It just occurred to me that my Rose will have some adjusting to do—no mother-in-law to occupy her time and no daughter to bounce in and out the cabin door."

"She'll be lonesome, you can bet," Katrina said. "Rattling about an empty nest can cause a mother to feel quite lost."

"Rose is a brave one, though," Pitt reassured himself. "You must remember, long ago she left her own mother in England to come to America. She has a strong will and the independent spirit that it takes to live in new frontiers. She'll be okay."

"Nonetheless," Watcher advised, "she deserves help in making yet another adjustment to her life. Don't you agree, Pitt?"

"Hmm. You are wise Watcher. Yes, I can see now that change will visit my life, too."

The fairies grew silent, each to their own thoughts.

Pitt felt challenged in serving Rose in this phase of her life. It had been a long time since anyone had really needed him.

Kate vacillated between serving old Hamlet and young John Clay Shuck and staying with Mack Riley, whom she had known since he was a boy in Kentucky.

Moreover, Keen wondered what she would do until Keren-happuck and Mack's daughter was born.

"It is time," Watcher said finally, "for us to prepare for the next generation."

PART FOUR

THE NEXT GENERATION

They watched animals drink at dusk ...
heard the birds sing evening vespers ...
& the haunting hoots of grandfather owls.

CHAPTER 17

CHANGE COMES TO SUGAR CREEK

It would take an anthologist to chronicle all the changes that came to the Riley Mill inhabitants following the loss of Grandmother Sparrow.

Neighbors remembered seeing the tall, slightly bent woman roam the wilds of the woods, collecting roots and plants that she used in herbal concoctions. She was the "old soul" that few had ever gotten to know since she came to America from Ireland when Keren was 15.

A recluse, Sparrow had lived an alternative existence. Aside from her own family to whom she was devoted, Sparrow was open with no one. Nonetheless, as mysterious as people viewed her personally, they treated her with uncommon respect for her healing prowess. Many a person had called upon her to cure what ailed them, knowing before they went that the only words she would utter would be directions for dosage. Sparrow simply waved off any attempt to pay her for her time or remedies. As outrageous as people thought she was, many would rather call on her, because of her successful treatments, than on her grandson-in-law, Mack Riley. Mack was aware of this, but he was, after all, new to the medical profession. "What could it hurt?" he reasoned. "It's only a few harmless herbs given by the vexatious old dear." Years later, in retrospect, he would allow that her decoctions and infusions were probably just as good as his bought and paid-for medicines.

And so, the days following her passing were hard, and the cause of her fatal injury would remain a mystery. Gradually, after the grieving, both individuals and families picked up the pieces and accepted the change in their lives.

The great loss of the medicine woman who had served them all brought forth the need for someone new to look after their health needs. Some felt that Sparrow might have pulled through with medications that are more modern; such as the quinine that Dr. Mack had wished for the night Sparrow passed. However, they looked now to Dr. Mack; it was time for change—the age of the pioneer doctor had come. Mack's dream was to open a clinic where he could have an up-to-date supply of medications, as well as a fully equipped medical office. By late fall, he found a perfect small clapboard house in nearby Edinburgh Village in which to set up his practice. He chose that location because he thought that it would draw patients from several communities, in addition to Riley's Mill. For the time being, he would travel back and forth from their cabin near the mill to his office. The days were long and busy. At the same time, Keren-happuck blossomed into a full-fledged pioneer wife as she made their house a home and started her own "medicinal" garden.

The nix, Katie, soon realized that Mack no longer looked to her for company or miracles. At first, she followed his buggy toward Edinburgh until she realized that the trip was too long for her to make every day. When he arrived home at night, it was always after dark; and he was too tired to pet her. He was much too busy with all the responsibility of his profession and being a husband to make time for Katrina. In the end, the fairy's decision between serving the Shucks and the Rileys was not a hard one to make. Mack was out.

That left the Shuck family. The child John Clay had a mother, a father, a grandfather and a grandmother to see to his every whim and the boy was quite content and well adjusted to frontier life. He did not really need a fairy guide other than to stimulate his imagination, which, of course, was extremely important to a child's mental health. On the other hand, Hamlet's free spirit and vagabond lifestyle seemed to have room for the likes of a nix. Moreover, to boot, the nix was a German fairy. She had been, after all, Hamlet's father's nix before she was a Riley nix.

Speaking of Grandfather Hamlet, he had chosen the next morning following the burying to return to his studio in the artist colony in Indianapolis. Samuel and the rest of the Shuck family had hoped he would close his shop and stay with them now that he knew whom his parents had been and his genealogy had been unraveled. Jon especially wanted his grandfather to stay for he had always loved the handsome old gentleman who came to visit from the city, but he had never really gotten to know very much about him. Hamlet's stories over the past few days had enraptured him and, in a way, he longed to follow the way of adventure that his grandfather had taken. Ah, but that was only a secret, pipe dream. Now that his two sons had been born, Jon's own, more practical desire was for four generations of Shucks to live and work together on the land. His grandfather, on the other hand, seemed bent on going back to his weaving.

Down at the O'Sheas, the woods seemed to be quieter these days. Rose and Shane had embraced new ventures from the time they were culture-crossed, lovelorn children on the river road going down to Carlingford town in Ireland to the time they immigrated to America. Now, they were at a crossroads once again and their renascent natures itched to blaze a new path. This time, their journey would be almost as exciting as those in the past, but much shorter—just across the yard. Rose wanted a new house. Shane couldn't wait to get started on it…

Truly, change was coming. Even in that corner of the Indiana woodland where time appears to stand still to this day, the great, silent meteor, Change, fell across Sugar Creek.

GRANNY ROSE AND GRANDPA BROWNIE

Rose and Shane had claimed their first cabin by "right of discovery" when they'd first ascended the ancient trail from the falls of the Ohio. In time, they had come to learn that the deserted long home was once the childhood home of the old Delaware midwife who had helped deliver and raise Keren-happuck—Stargazer. Soon after Grandmother Sparrow crossed over to join her ancestors and Keren-happuck married Dr. Mack, Rose was back to re-feathering her nest, but it was now a lonesome nest. She needed a change, a spark, and Shane knew just what to do.

"Come outside, Rosie," he said one evening. "I want to show you something."

Rose was hot and tired and was just about to sit down to rest for the evening. She had spent the afternoon making new red gingham curtains for the house. "What is it, dear? I'm as tired as an old dog. Can it wait?"

"It can't wait," he said rather urgently. Rose took note of his tone of voice and decided that her rocking chair could wait for a few minutes more. Taking down her old green shawl, the same one she wore on her first crossing of the Atlantic into New York harbor, she stepped wearily out to see what was so important.

Shane took her hand and started across the yard through the sleeping wild-flowers between the house and the high bank over the bend in Sugar Creek.

Pitt was standing in the slit in the old sycamore and decided to follow along. "Hmm," he muttered, as his misty figure tripped through the dew that had already started to settle the day. "Where in the cat hair are they going?"

When the couple was about 30 feet from the edge of the bank, Shane stopped and looked down. Rose, naturally, looked down, too. At the tips of their shoes lay a line of twig sticks stretching both ways from the spot where they stood. Upon further inspection, Rose could see that it formed a large rectangle and branched out into more rectangles. "What is it?"

"It's our new house," Shane said, a huge smile spreading across his face.

"A new house?" Rose gasped. "How did you know? I have dreamed of a new house of my own, not one that somebody else had before us?"

"Oh! I don't know. Maybe it's the way you sigh every time you sweep that tired old floor in the cabin or the way you pour over the advertisements in your Ladies' Magazine from Boston. It's time we get updated, m'love."

"My goodness! It sounds wonderful, but I would miss the old cabin. After all, Keren was born there and..."

"Okay," Shane laughed. "We'll keep the old cabin and you can visit it anytime you want; but it's high time you had a floor big enough for one of Uncle Hamlet's beautiful tapestry rugs—like the one Samuel and Abigail have."

"But, is it practical to have two houses? After all, there's just the two of us left."

"Is that what you think? Only two of us left. You make it sound like the end of the world. Don't you know that our household is already starting to grow? By this time next year, I wouldn't be surprised if we have a new grandchild. You'll be a granny, Rose! Mack says he wants to have a dozen!

"Now don't get the cart before the mare, Shane!"

"Well, I'm sure we'll find a use for the old house; in fact, why not use it as a guest house?

"I'm thinking that Keren and Mack will move to Edinburgh when the practice gets going and there will be times they will want to stay over. The village is growing and they'll be glad to get out of the hustle and bustle to the cool woods."

"Yes!" Rose finally agreed. "We can give the old cabin to Keren to use as a summer home!"

"A summer home then," Shane said. "We'll be regular real estate barons!"

"Oh...my...gosh!" Pitt breathed in astonishment, as he stood hidden in the grass beside Rose. "A dozen grandchildren? Oh, my aching feet! I can already feel my sore tootsies from running after them!

"Oh, Watcher...Yoo-hoo! You'll never guess..." Pitt squealed as he made a beeline for the enchanted tree. "I'm going to be a grandfather brownie!"

*   *   *

The house raising was an exciting event in the Riley Mill community. All the neighboring settlers came to help build the new home for the O'Sheas: the Henry's, the Shuck's, the Riley's, the Johnson's, the Thompson's, the Scott's, and the Adams's, to name a few who had settled along the banks of Sugar Creek. Even the Duckworth's, the Brown's and the Needham's from upstream lent their hands and tools. In no time, Rose and Shane were sitting out evenings on their new porch over the high bank directly over Sugar Creek watching all the happenings along the water. They waved at neighbors and strangers alike who traveled Sugar Creek, and heard any news called up from people in every class of transport from canoes to flat boats. They watched the animals drink at dusk before returning to the woods to rest. Most of all, they enjoyed the birds as they sang evening vespers amid the haunting hoots of the grandfather woods owls.

All they needed now was that grandbaby...

Red Key

Suddenly, Katrina was starved. Together the nixes finished off two bowls of the feature stew and chased it down with pints of freshly brewed root beer -- a specialty of the Red Key.

Chapter 18

Katrina's Choice

Katrina still hadn't completely resolved her dilemma about whether to stay with Jon Clay or go to Hamlet. There was, of course, a great temptation to put off the decision, sleep late and lounge around the sycamore all day. For the time being, the American Spirits had settled into quite a monotonous routine of quiet days and uneventful evening fairy rings. It was a time of rest while each spirit geared up for the next round of souls and situations to come into their keep.

Tall yellow sneezeweed, with its drooping daisy-like flower heads, covered the woods as autumn grew its choice of wildflowers. The fairies sat in their crackling fire ring sneezing and complaining about the effects of the plant as it became brittle and powdery in late fall.

"I remember when Miss Sparrow used to come out about this time of year to collect dry sneezeweed to use for making snuff," Keen reminisced. "It was nearly impossible to breathe in the loft while she crushed it."

"I know," Katrina agreed as she sat on a log, in her true nix fairy form, beside the banshee. "It always makes my eyes water—especially when I transfigure into a dog."

"I say," Pitt said. "Why do humans use snuff, anyway?"

"To make them sneeze, of course," Keen said sarcastically.

Pitt gave her one of those 'oh, ha, ha!' looks and continued. "Old Baron Caine and his English aristocrats used to carry an expensive sneezing powder in little gold tins. It smelled just like dry sneezeweed. Rose's mother used to offer it after a meal because she didn't want pipe smoke smelling up the house. She rather liked the stuff, herself."

"How on earth did sneezeweed replace a pipe?" Pitt inquired.

"I think it is how high society gentry take their tobacco," Katrina answered. "I suppose they use dried tobacco to clear their sinuses, like we use sneezeweed to clear ours."

"For sure, it does that," Keen allowed; "but Sparrow made snuff to give people for headaches, insomnia, and toothaches. She used it for lots of ailments. I remember her giving it to treat a cough or a bad cold and then giving it to everyone else in the household, sick or not, as a measure against contagion."

"How very curious," Watcher surmised after listening to the conversation of the fairies, "for human beings to have such an appetite for a weed we simply abhor!

"Ka-choo!"

The group fell quiet for a time, and then Katrina gave a long, audible sigh. "Hmm…not to change the subject, but I've been thinking about going up to the city to check on Hamlet. Any of you want to go with me?"

Pitt's interest peaked. "I told Keen just today that I bet your German curiosity about Grandfather Shuck would get the best of you."

"Uh, yes, actually, it has."

"What about that little kid, though?" Pitt asked. "Who's going to look after John Clay if you go?"

"I didn't say I was going to stay. Just thought I'd go visit the man, see how he's doing, and see *what* he's doing…"

Pitt looked over at Keen. "I told you she'd go up there! Didn't I, Keeny?" Looking all around the fairy ring, he spoke to the group as a whole: "I told Keen she'd go!"

"Really, Pitt," Keen objected to his gloating. "What's the big deal anyway? Isn't anyone allowed to leave the woods? You'd think it was a crime!

"And, no, Kate, I think this is a trip you need to make alone. It should be of your own free will whether you join Grandfather Hamlet or stay here with Jon Clay."

"Hmm," Kate considered. "I suppose you're right. "I thought I'd leave in the morning; just wanted to let you know."

When Katrina arrived at Hamlet's shop, he was not at home. She took the time to explore his quarters and get to know the nooks and crannies of living such an existence, should she decide to stay. "Hmm," she murmured as she scurried about. "Lots of warm lint piles and tapestry rolls in which to snuggle in the winter…no sneezeweed about…no wet forest grass to navigate; and, yes, loaves of bread to nibble anytime I feel hungry. I wonder…looks tempting…."

The nix waited all morning for Hamlet to come home. At noon, she made a meal of the end of a loaf of rye bread. She was almost asleep in the front window, where she sat watching for him, when he walked up the front stoop and opened the door. Startled, Kate tumbled off the sill and fell with a thud onto a stack of books on the floor beside the divan. Hamlet was carrying a sheet of parchment with an order for a new tapestry on it. She watched him stand his walking stick in the corner beside the door, place the paper down on a secretary, where he obviously kept his records, and then walk into the small pantry kitchen. "Best to keep quiet for a while," she thought to herself. "Don't want to make myself known too soon. He may not take to the likes of a nix after spending so many years with those pirates when he was a child."

After eating a light meal, Hamlet returned to the secretary and spent the afternoon sketching an intricate design for the commissioned tapestry. Kate was interested to note that the weaver smoked a pipe; did not use snuff. A sweet-smelling cherry tobacco odor from Hamlet's pipe filled the room. She rather liked the aroma of his smoke rings as they rose like circular kites toward the ceiling. "Such a pleasant, grandfathery essence," she mused. It was all so warm and comfortable—this weaver's studio of Hamlet's. "I could get used to it very easily." She took the nap she had started while he scratched away with quill and parchment.

THE RED KEY

Evening brought quite another side of Hamlet's life. Near dark, he put on a purple felt hat with a long fluffy feather that streamed down his neck, picked up his walking stick and started out the door into the wooden sidewalk where gas flares twinkled in lampposts to light up the whole street. Kate was right at his heel when he closed the door. "Close!" she panted. "Almost clipped my wing!" She hid herself in the riot of plumes on his hat and wondered where they were going.

Much in the cadence of a routine, Hamlet stopped off to make his daily deposit at the little bank situated only a few doors from his own. "Evening, Hamlet," said the bespectacled teller as he took the purse of money from him.

"Evening, Mr. Squibbit."

The two exchanged no other words while the teller counted the money, put it in a drawer, and wrote out a receipt, which he put back in the well-worn moneybag. "Good evening, Sir."

"Good evening."

Katrina made a mental note: "Men of few words," while she rode comfortably along in the purple accessory.

Hamlet continued down the walk until he reached the end of the street where, above him, a sign reading "The Red Key" clinked against its chain as though it were welcoming passersby. He turned toward the door, took the two steps down, and ducked his head to miss the low transom above it. Kate held on for dear life as her perch bowed toward the floor upon his entry into his favorite haunt. Once in, he nearly squashed her while removing the macaroni head covering and placing it beside him on the bench he took.

The room held the oddest, most colorful assortment of men and women, curmudgeons and dames, the nix had ever witnessed. They were artists, of course—Hamlet's friends. Each of them was wearing a costume of dress peculiar to his or her profession or talent. The woodworkers wore leather to repel splinters, while sawdust swam off their tousled heads in waves. A pair of tinsmiths sat together with matching scarlet shirts to belie the smudges of blood from cut fingers, the hazard of their occupation. Fine artists wore smocks stained with all the colors of a rainbow that matched their multi-color skin. Dancers—both students and instructors—undulated their sleek, muscular figures to reach their usual seats. All alike, young and old, were talking or laughing at once as they lifted glasses and scraped spoons across pewter plates full of the evening's fare, in what seemed to Kate to be pure bedlam. For a few moments, the nix wanted to escape the din and go straight back to the quiet, plain forest of pioneer life. Soon, however, she noticed how happy everyone was. Perhaps there was more to the picture here than met the eye. Surely, Grandfather Hamlet wouldn't come to such a place unless there was something more.

Gradually, through the noise, she began to feel it—the sweet spirit of the place. The artists were genuinely glad to see each other, to ask about the other's day and to share an evening meal together. Oh! To be sure, some talked more than others did, but all enjoyed the society of friends in the otherwise lonely world of the dedicated artist. Some were unwashed and unshaven from a day's toil, but each of them was accepted for himself in a room that a larger world would not understand.

People packed the gathering place as they relaxed, ate and drank their favorite ales. A long bar ran the length of one side of the tavern, while wooden tables and benches filled the rest of the room. Barmaids worked the main dining area carrying food and drink to the regulars, while a tall, clean-shaven, well-built bartender built stouts and poured drinks for the counter group, as well as the diners. Through a pair of swinging doors at the back of the establishment,

Katrina saw the cook in his tall white baker's cap scurrying about a steaming kitchen and stopping to laugh at the trifles of the barmaids. He was a jolly specimen who looked very comfortable dipping up stews, pulling bread out of his stone oven, and tossing various and sundry vegetables and desserts onto the gray metal platters.

FRIEDRICH

Kate actually began to enjoy the ambience of the friendly tavern and ignored the loud talking until it sounded like the drone of bagpipe music in the background. She was certainly too excited to think of eating, so she began to study the revelers, to try to guess who they were, what they did, and the place of their origin. Her eye came to rest on a figure sitting on the very last stool at the bar. "Now, there's an extremely sour person," she thought. He didn't seem to be having conversation with anyone and had a deep scowl on his face as his ale sloshed out onto the bar and his clothing each time he lifted his glass. Then, just for a moment, she thought she saw him disappear. A blink and he was back. "What on earth?" she started. "This will take some closer scrutiny." For the first time, she slipped out of the tangled feather and flitted across the room to where the dour little man was sitting and perched beside him on the bar counter. She realized at once that it was no ordinary man; it was a curmudgeonly old nix—a male of her own genre.

"Hello, mate!"

"Er…a…what?" he growled and glanced toward her.

"I said, hello."

"Who are you," he grunted. "Go away."

"I'm Katrina from the Schwarzwald. It's just so unusual to see a fellow nix in America."

"Hmm. Suppose it is. How did you get in here anyway? This is an unlikely place for a nix."

"What do you mean? You are a nix, aren't you? I might add a rather sad representation of a nix."

"Humph!" he cleared his throat. "I beg your pardon." He resumed his gaze at the bar in front of him and added, "What's it to ya?"

"Maybe nothing." Katrina was starting to take quite an interest in the new-found nix. "I am, however, certainly curious about a mate who appears to be having rather of a rough go of it. To whom do you belong? Are you lost? Is there anything I can do for you?"

The nix set down his glass and looked sideways at the nuisance beside him. "As a matter of fact—I am lost."

Katrina gave him her undivided attention and waited for him to go on.

"Well," he began with a little more civility toward her. "The family I crossed with came from Heidelberg. They escaped up the Rhine to Amsterdam, like so many other small farmers, and took passage to America on an English emigrant boat. They were promised land by the Crown and headed across Indiana to take possession of it. While they were crossing a river, the whole wagon overturned in the current and every one of them drowned."

"So what did you do?"

"I wandered around for a long time trying to find someone who needed a German house fairy. Each household I visited seemed to be quite settled in its own way—none of which included the need for a nix."

"Oh, dear," Kate lamented. "Now I understand why you've become so destitute. Time is running out for you, isn't it?"

A word of explanation is necessary here. Three catastrophes can befall a nix. One is that at the end of a family assignment, a nix can become obsolete and extinguished. Secondly, when a territorial dispute between two home fairies occurs, the King and Queen may opt to remove one of them to another family or to eliminate the sprite. Thirdly, at the end of one of Earth's Ages, Oberon and Titania realign and cull many of the fairies. The male nix was close to this sort of tragic demise; he was treading on extinction ice, prime for permanent disappearance.

"Time," the despondent nix repeated apprehensively, "is, indeed, running out. I wonder how long I have. Already, I fade in and out, you see. After the accident, I drifted for weeks until I fell in with this artist colony. I found that I could hang out and nobody really noticed, or cared, at least. I seemed to fit in with them to a degree, because they are definitely more bohemian than the average American. Let me put it this way: these people are more tolerant of the occasional brief apparition of an off-course German fairy in their midst, but there really is no honest reason for me to be here."

"I see," Kate said pensively. "Tell you what. Maybe I can help you. You seem like a nice enough fellow, you're just down on your luck."

The unfortunate nix suddenly became aware of his slovenly appearance and tried to slick down his errant mop of hair to look a little more respectable. It didn't help much, but the meaning of the gesture was not lost on Katrina. "Well, cousin. Do you mind if I call you cousin?"

The nix shook his head numbly.

"Say!" she suddenly realized. "I don't know your name!"

"Friedrich."

"Excellent! A good strong German name!

"Now, Friedie," Kate went on in a much more casual tone than before. "I think you can help me almost as much as I can help you. I have a problem, too. I guess that's one of the reasons I, myself, am here tonight."

Friedrich listened while Kate told him her whole tangled past about first belonging to Herr Shuck in Germany and then finding the Riley family in America, only to once again find herself back with the Shucks of Sugar Creek. She related the details of the decision she must make between Grandfather Shuck and young Jon Clay.

"So you see," she concluded. "I can't be both places and I don't know what to do."

"And," Friedrich took over the rhetoric, "you want me to take one of them?"

"Exactly. However, I don't know which you would be best suited for—the old man or the child. I am inclined to think Hamlet, from the condition I find you in; but I guess I really rather hoped to join him here, myself. I wish I knew what his future plans are."

"I think I can help you there," Friedrich offered. "Your old German is planning to return to the mountain where he was born. I heard him tell someone just last night that as soon as he finishes a new piece that he promised someone, he'll leave."

"Indeed?"

"Indeed."

"So his quest continues…that does put a new slant on things. If he is bound for Germany, I must guide him along the way. He is a long way from finding all the answers for which he is looking. I know that, now.

"So, how are you with little boys, Fried?"

"Fit and able," the nixie replied. "It was two boys I served until the river took them. I think you will be surprised at how capable I really am under positive circumstances! Again, he patted down his hair, this time raising his hood over it. "Besides that, you're giving me my last chance. Do you think I'd blow that?"

"I believe you. It's a deal then?"

"It's a deal."

Suddenly Katrina felt hungry. Together the nixes finished off two bowls of Friday stew and chased them down with pints of freshly brewed root beer—a specialty of the Red Key.

CHAPTER 19

GRANDFATHER'S LETTER

Katrina didn't really want to go back to the farm yet; she hadn't gotten to spend much time with Hamlet. Nevertheless, she knew that she would have to get Friedrich settled in—make sure he would even work out—before she and Hamlet left for Germany. Besides, it would be a few weeks before he could complete the tapestry and get ready to leave. She and Friedrich went to the farm.

"Did you ever wonder why no one ever started a church here?" Abigail Shuck asked her daughter-in-law, Jesse, one afternoon. The two were quilting beneath the trees in Jesse's back yard while the baby and John Clay took their naps on an old quiltlet spread beside their chairs.

"Well, no. But it sure would be nice to have one within walking distance, wouldn't it?"

"Now that John Clay is getting a little older," Abigail said, "it would be a good thing to get him started going to Sunday school. He could meet some of the other children his age and make some friends.

"Samuel said something last night about a new church being built between here and Amity Crossing, said he heard it at the mill when he went down there to get some corn ground for the chickens."

"Who's building it?" Jesse asked idly as she ran her needle down and up through the muslin.

"It's the Presbyterians from Franklin. I guess the congregation can't agree on things, and they're splitting up."

"Things like what?"

"Oh. You know. Different ideas about the worship service, some have one idea and others have another—and, slavery. You know that's a big issue everywhere, I guess."

"I never thought about that. Nobody around here has slaves: the North outlawed it years ago. My folks used to, though, down in Kentucky; but, since I came up here and married Jon, I just don't think about having slaves."

"Uh-huh. My dad had slaves who helped sow tobacco and did work around the place. I remember how they would go out and plant the tobacco beads in ashes in the fencerow in the early spring; and then when the plants got big enough, they would transplant them in the patch. Dad had several workhorses and the slaves would always take care of them, too.

"Then, we had Mammy Lucy. She took care of us kids."

"I had a Mammy, too," Jesse said. "Sure seems like a long time ago."

"Oh, well. Sam said they are going to call it the Highland Presbyterian Church, and they are going to have all kinds of revivals and things to get people coming. You know Maggie Riley, don't you?"

"Yes, Mack's mom."

"Right. She's one of the main ones leaving the church in town to start the new one."

"Oh, she is? I always liked her. Maybe we could go down there sometime after they get it built. It's a lot closer than town."

"That's just what I was thinking."

Friedrich and Katrina were taking the whole conversation in from a gardenia bush in the back yard next to the clothesline. They had arrived that morning and decided to go straight to the Shucks so Friedrich could get a good look at the little ones he would be watching. After that, Kate planned to show him around the neighborhood. The fairy ring that night would be soon enough to introduce the new nix to the rest of the sprites.

"Well," Kate asked. "What do you think?"

"I guess I can't tell for sure, yet. The babies are asleep. But from where I stand, it beats traveling in a covered wagon across a flooded river!"

"You'll like these people. Salt of the earth. Little John Clay is smart as a tack and he will give you a run for your money, but he will be loads of fun to help grow up.

"Come on, let's go. We got a lot of ground to cover before dark."

The nixes flew off like two butterflies and made a fly-by over the quilters and the sleeping tots so that Friedrich could have a clearer look.

A Letter from Grandfather Hamlet

The letter held news that was not at all to Samuel and Jon Shuck's liking.

...I will take the stage and stop by before I leave. I thought, if it was okay, I'd leave my looms in the barn because I don't know when I'll be coming back this way...

The letter, indeed, had not held good news. Grandfather Shuck was not getting any younger. When would he ever stop looking for whatever it was that kept him so unsettled? That was the question on Abigail and Jesse's minds, too; although they would never be so bold as to pry; grandson Jon could not let the question rest.

"Maybe if I go with him, he'll come back to stay," he argued with his dad.

"No, Jon. You have a family to look after, a farm to work. My father always has been a loner and I do not want you to become like him. No matter where he goes, I don't think he'll ever be satisfied with settling down someplace."

"But he gave me his silver fob! Somehow, I feel responsible for him now. I don't know why, I just do!"

"Why? It is just a piece of jewelry. He gave it to you as a gift, that's all," Samuel argued.

"No. I'm sorry Dad, I cannot agree. I know I am supposed to go with him for some reason. Shouldn't someone look after him?"

"Son. I believe you already are like him. Traveling shoes. I had hoped I'd never see this day."

Jon could see the anguish in his father's face. "I promise, Dad. I'll come back just as soon as I can; and, if God's willing, I'll bring back Grandfather, too."

"What does Jesse think about all this? Have you even asked her what she thinks? Two kids! Jon! Two kids!"

"She's fine with it, now," he answered softly, remembering the argument he had had with her about it.

Samuel looked into Jon's face and said a little sarcastically, "Yes. I'm sure she's delighted."

"No, really, she's okay with it."

"See? I told you so," Pitt said to Keen in the fairy ring. *They are really gonna need our Katrina now. Two going! I hope this Friedrich is all he seems to be...."*

Feldberg Mountain

Four months later...

The old German woman stood outside her doorstep with a homemade round broom, which she had tied together with a red ribbon. "What? Whom did you say? I don't hear so well anymore."

It was a beautiful day on the mountain. Hamlet and Jon had eaten an early breakfast of scones and coffee at the inn that morning and learned of the woman who had lived below Feldberg for 70 years.

"Johann and Gertrude von Shuck," young Jon explained. "My grandfather's parents. We hear they used to live on the mountain. He made violins...Herr Johann von Shuck. Did you know him? My grandfather, here, was born up there."

The warm wind blew strands of gray and white hair, which were trying to escape from under her day bonnet, while the woman looked up toward the top of the ancient rock peak called Feldberg. Her periwinkle eyes lit up after a moment. "Violin? Yes, I know of him.... He lives way up the mountain there," she said pointing up a narrow road. "Dead, you know?"

"Yes," Jon smiled. "We know."

"Go on, then. You find his old house."

The haunting gray chalet stood in ruins—a cold, unpainted skeleton. Grass and tares had grown up around its windows and doors and, long since, buried the stepping-stones to the door.

"It must have been built well over a hundred years ago, certainly before the turn of the 18th Century," Hamlet thought. He wondered whether his own grandfather had made plans at a supper table somewhere in Germany to raise the family dwelling on Feldberg. He imagined a conversation spoken in old Deutsch about the work being hard, but the reward of the new von Shuck home, well-made and strong, being sweet. It would rise in a fresh woods clearing and bring celebration to an otherwise silent awareness of progress. A hundred years of yesterdays—each one visited by torrents of rain, six-inch snowfalls and the rays of a scalding sun above the Black Forest—had taken their toll on the still imposing structure that once lifted a shining new face toward the tree-tops—a cathedral to passersby.

Hamlet's mood waxed back in time as he imagined his own father as a boy finding refuge in a straw-filled tick in the loft when blackness had fallen on the mountain. When Johann had grown, he would long remember his peaceful bed in the aerie above the vaulted, rotunda-like central room from which the business of everyday living fingered.

"To think! Sparrow and I lived here, could have been raised here," Hamlet daydreamed. "Ah, but a century has passed since those walls went up—four hundred seasons gone. Just look at the weeds and ruin—disgusting, for it's old now."

The soul of the old house entered the old weaver's heart as he looked through a broken window—an eye into the past. Then, stepping back, Hamlet thought, "Poor, lonesome old home; its body is wrinkled and its window eyes are saggy and sad."

Hamlet thought he saw his childhood chalet sigh the breath of life. "It could live again. Who knows?"

The graveyard had to be there somewhere. The old woman had told them so. Presently, they saw the crumbling rock walls of an old cemetery behind the house. Hamlet saw the marker first; and then Jon hurried over to see it. It read:

Gertrude Shuck
Beloved wife
Departed this life to rest
1799.

Hamlet could not speak. He just could not find words. He had been looking for so very long. Now, he stared like a statue at the inscription. A huge lump rose in his throat.

"You've found your mother, Grandfather," Jon finally said, taking the old man's arm.

"I have," Hamlet answered, "but where is my father?"

"He has to be around here someplace," Jon said walking a bit farther.

Jon and Hamlet continued searching through the weeds to find a second stone. It didn't take them long in such a tiny graveyard to find that there was no second stone. The only stone, at all, was that of Hamlet's mother.

"Maybe he's buried someplace else, Grandfather."

"I guess so," Hamlet said flatly.

"Let's go back down to see if the German lady knows where he is," Jon suggested. "We can keep an eye out for other tombstones on our way back down."

The two walked back down the dusty road, sweating now from the noonday sun. Insects flirted around them trying to find fresh nectar beneath the perspiration. The rosy-cheeked woman, this time, was inside just starting her noon meal.

"Oh! Now I remember…He goes away to America. He leaves his mountain."

"Do you know where he went in America?" Jon asked.

"No; but he leave his mountain."

"Thank you for all your help," Hamlet said and bowed to the woman. "What is your name, by the way, Ma'am?"

"I am Gisela Puck," she said with a ready smile.

"I am Hamlet Shuck and this is my grandson, Jon."

Hamlet tipped his felt hat, which was now minus the long feather that he wore in the artist's colony, to her and she, in turn, gave him a small curtsy.

"Good-bye, Frau Puck," Jon said, tipping his own hat. "Thank you very much for your help."

The two men went back over to the inn for some lunch, themselves. "Now what, Grandfather?"

"Well, I was just thinking there may be ship passenger lists somewhere on file. After we eat, we'll find a constable and put the question to him."

Just so you'll know, Katrina had taken the time to find her clan while Jon and Hamlet trekked up and down the mountain. It was a happy homecoming and the nixes begged their American cousin to tell them all about that faraway land. She talked way into the late afternoon about the American Spirits and the newfound American nix, Friedrich, whom some of them, it turned out, knew. It was a good visit, but she was glad that she lived in America where each day brought some new adventure. The German nixes were definitely an old time, old-world bunch. She couldn't wait to get back to Indiana.

Charles Town, South Carolina

Four months later.

"The passenger list definitely said 'Destination: Charles Town by way of Amsterdam,'" Hamlet told the pudgy woman with orange cheeks behind the desk at the Port Authority Office. "We both—my grandson and I—saw it!"

"Well, maybe it did, but I have no record of a Herr Shuck having been on that ship. At least he didn't report to our office if he was on it."

"But, it said…" Hamlet continued to argue with the clerk who was losing her patience fast.

"Mister. What do you want me to do? I said he isn't on this piece of paper!"

Each of the matron's three chins rose and fell as she stabbed the parchment with the ragged orange claw of her index finger. Jon had never seen such a heavily made-up woman before and he thought she looked like an outrageous, overgrown calico cat.

"Come on, Grandfather," he begged. "She doesn't know."

Hamlet was still not ready to give up, but he knew that they were going to get no place with this person. "Okay. We can go, but my father did not just disappear into thin air, did he?

"Do you suppose he died on the ship?"

"No, Grandfather. She looked that up, too. He was not among the three people who died on board."

They had just about reached the exit when the woman with orange cheeks called out to them across the big room. "Sirs! Excuse me! Sirs!" she bellowed over her desk. Jon and Hamlet stopped and turned around to see if she meant them.

"Mr. Shuck! Would you please come back?"

"Yes?" Hamlet said as they reached the desk.

"I just thought of something," she said and flopped back down in her chair out of breath.

"The port clinic," she said. "Sometimes, people who are ill when they arrive are taken to the clinic. Why don't you try there? It's just a thought, but you could ask."

"Yes. Thank you. Where is this clinic?"

"Just up the street. You will see it. It'll say 'Charles Town Public Clinic.'"

"Yes!" Kate shouted. "Yes! Yes! Yes! Finally!" The nix would have had quite a task on her hands if she'd had to make an appearance in order to explain the whereabouts of her old master.

Walking into the rather shabby, clearly old, medical building, Jon and Hamlet had only reserved hope that they would find any information in this less than sanitary facility.

"We do have a list, by year, of immigrant patients who come here off the ships," another unkempt, lipsticked lady told them. "Here. You can go over it yourself, if you want."

"Another list," Hamlet thought. "Please.... Let his name be on this one," and took the yellowed document over to a table to inspect it. Jon stood beside him as he ran his finger down the pages until he came to the year 1800. "There," he said. "That's the year after the date on your mother's tombstone. Start there!"

The writing was poor, even faded in some places until one could hardly read it. Jon was saying the names on the list as Hamlet came to them. "Stultz...von

Stralendorff...Schmidt...Himmelberger...SHUCK! That's it! Grandfather! That is it! Johann von Shuck!"

"Shuck," Hamlet said softly. "Shuck...yes, there it is. So it looks like he made it to America, after all."

"Can you believe we finally found him, Grandfather?"

Hamlet just stared at the page with a huge smile. He could not stop staring. It was almost too good to be true. Then, he remembered himself. "But, what happened to him after he came here?"

"Does it say someplace?" Jon asked taking the ledger. "No, not on here, at least. Let's ask if there's a way to find out."

"No," the lady said. "That's the only old record we have, but sometimes, if they die here, we bury them in the public burial yard out back."

"Thank you," Jon said and quickly took his grandfather by the hand. "We'll look." With that, they left the sickly stale air of the office and stepped out into the fresh sea breeze.

They found the grave marker in a while. It read, *J. Shuck, Germany, 1800.* Both looked at it with a sort of blank stare. So that was it. They had reached the end. Strangely, it felt rather anticlimactic compared to finding the grave of Frau Gertrude on Feldberg. Neither knew quite what to say.

"He's here," Jon finally said.

"Yes...he is."

Something didn't feel right...to either of them. That night, in the Charles Town Inn, each had his own thoughts and planned an agenda around them.

The genealogy traced, Jon felt that Hamlet had no excuse not to go back with him. The quest was over. It had to be because Hamlet had found his parents and his home. He'd found his sister. What more could there be? The quest should have been over, but there was still a little fog in the path.

One thing was for sure, it was time to go home to Indiana as far as Jon was concerned. He had been away from Jesse and the boys long enough. He had crossed the ocean with Grandfather Hamlet, climbed Feldberg Mountain with him, and seen the resting places of both his great-grandmother and his great-grandfather. He had had the adventure of his young life and come to love his grandfather even better.

It was true that he had gotten to know a little bit more about his family, but had Jon actually gotten to *know* Hamlet better? He didn't think so; but he had had a glimpse into the hidden country of that rare old soul—a land designed by life's experiences. Jon was beginning to realize that each day he, himself, was trailblazing a private country of his own.

HAMLET'S QUEST ISN'T OVER

The feeling of closure, which Hamlet thought he would have if he *found* his family, was just not there. Sleep usually came easily to the gentle, aging weaver; but, upon this night, questions filled the man's senses. "Why was there no record of my father's belongs? Surely, he had baggage of some kind.

"And, why is the place he owned on Feldberg in ruins and the chalet still standing vacant? Am I the heir to that piece of land on that beautiful mountain?"

He wondered, also, about the old German woman that lived at the bottom of the road up to the Shuck chalet. She was up in years and seemed to be somewhat forgetful and daft. Perhaps there was a lot more to Herr Shuck's leaving the mountain than she had told them.

"Maybe," he thought, "there are still records of the cartage loaded onto the ship in which Father made his passage to America."

All these things swam past his half-closed eyes like quiet hallucinations in the time between half awake and deep sleep—those imagined episodes where sometimes problems are solved. In his mind, Hamlet saw his silver watch fob—the one that matched his sister's pendant; then, he saw his father's fiddle that hung on Shane's cabin wall. In the middle of the crazy fleeting visions, Hamlet saw himself standing on Feldberg before his restored ancestral home, in its original colorful, Deutsch beauty. His breathing became easier and a look of peace came over his face while his eyes closed completely. He knew what to do....

LEAVING CHARLES TOWN

Hamlet was quiet during breakfast the next morning. Jon made idle conversation with the server and ate a hearty last meal at the inn before starting the journey home. Hamlet picked at his meat and drank two cups of coffee while his grandson prattled on about the trip back. After he was finished, Jon said, "Come on, Grandfather. Let's go home."

Only then did Hamlet lower the boom. "I'm not going back to Indiana. I'm going to Amsterdam and then back to Germany."

"What? Why? We found your parents; the mystery of your beginnings is solved!"

"To a point. I still have unanswered questions."

"But, Grandfather!" Jon said in a slightly irritated tone. "One of the reasons I wanted to come with you was to make sure you came back! What else do you need to know?"

"I know you want me to go back with you, but I haven't come this far just to go home when there are things I want to know more about. I cannot expect you to understand—you have a family waiting for you back in Indiana, where you belong. They are your world."

Jon was exasperated. "But you are my family, too; you are part of my world—you are a part of Dad's world! Why go back to Germany when so many love you at home?"

"That's just it, Grandson. I know about the love of my own child and grand-children; I do not doubt it one minute. Nevertheless, I want to know more about the lives of my father and mother. I want to know what they were like, who they were, and how they lived."

"You do realize, don't you, Grandfather, that you are not getting any younger? What if we never see you again?"

"Honey," Hamlet said to his grandson with all the affection he would dis-play for a small child, "I'll see you again. However, even if I do not, you must know that as long as I live, wherever I am, I will love you and all the rest of my family, as well as my friends. I have had a good, happy life because of each and every one of you."

Hamlet reached in his vest and took out the silver fob. "I want to give this back to you, now. I am finished with its magic; it brought me home. Someday you will pass it on to John Clay. It belongs in the family. Perhaps there will be more magic in it yet."

"The only magic that I want right now is for you to come home with me," Jon lamented.

"You *know* you have Jesse and the boys to carry on the family circle, secure in the knowledge of who you are and where you belong. I have never had that. I have been a vagabond most of my life. I'm still hunting my own knowledge."

Jon took his grandfather's silver treasure and placed it in his own vest pocket. "You won't change your mind, then—even if I beg?"

Hamlet looked long and lovingly at Jon. "I'll walk you to the stage."

"...An old cemetery behind the house.
Hamlet saw the marker first ..."

CHAPTER 20

UNANSWERED QUESTIONS

Katrina had no trouble in deciding to stay with Hamlet.

"I want to disinter my father and arrange to have him shipped home to Germany for burial in the family plot," Hamlet explained to a familiar face, his usual clerk in the Charles Town Public Clinic.

"You're kidding!"

"No. I'm absolutely serious."

"So you did find your father in the lot?"

"I did, thanks to you."

"Well," the surprised woman said. "That's the first time anybody ever wanted to dig someone up outta there. I am not sure how to arrange that. I'll have to ask."

Hamlet waited while the bewildered woman disappeared behind a partition with bar-protected windows. He was feeling rather pleased with himself that he had thought of sending his father's remains back to Feldberg Mountain. "If nothing else," he had thought to himself, "my parents will be together again on the mountain."

He thought of Sparrow, his twin sister, resting in the Riley Mill Cemetery. "I think she would have wanted me to do this."

Katrina was pleased that the Grandfather's quest had led him this far. She wanted to tell him so, to talk with him; but the old man had never known about his father's nix—that Mack Riley's dog was really the Shuck family's nix. She was a Shuck again and knew that she would never transform into a dog again. She was a nix, and as a German fairy would no longer have to disguise her existence—at least as a dog

AMSTERDAM

The question of Johann's missing personal belongings led Hamlet to backtrack his father's route to America.

The port of departure office in Amsterdam had in its archives a list of all German emigrants who had chosen that route through Holland in the late 1700s to remove to America. Hamlet was given to understand there that most of the many German emigrants from the Black Forest had been forced to escape the grips of the dark lords in the country in secret, by night, by floating up the Rhine River in tiny, low boats. It was a time of general warfare between the low farmers and the landowners. His father, on the other hand, had been a wood-carver—an instrument maker—and, as such, traveled as a gentleman.

And it was as a gentleman, indeed, that Herr Johann von Shuck had boarded the *Wooden Shoe* for America. His quarters were the best: a stateroom above the general holding area for the lower class in the belly of the ship.

"Yes," the official at the emigrant office in Amsterdam said. "The gentleman was assigned to the Drinker State Room. He checked in, as baggage, one sea chest."

"Could you tell me," Hamlet asked, "whether that chest was still on board when the Wooden Shoe returned to its home port? My father was ill aboard the ship when it reached Charles Town and taken to the sick clinic. There is no record of any property that he may have had upon arrival."

"I'm afraid I have no idea about that sort of thing. That was a long time ago. We do have a lost and found room. You could check there."

"No," said the man in charge of missing baggage. "We have no lost luggage with that name on it. You might try the port office in Bremen. Most international travelers on the Rhine who come up from the Black Forest register there."

FRAU GISELA'S MEMORY

The stage ride to Feldberg down the Rhine seemed like it would never end. Hamlet just hoped that the crate holding his father's remains would be there when he arrived. It shipped from Charles Town separately to the Feldberg undertaker according to maritime mandates. He was glad to find that, indeed, the crate had arrived and was waiting there. He would have to check on his father's old trunk later. Hamlet made arrangements to have the burial the next day, and then walked over to Frau Puck's to invite her to accompany him up the mountain for the bittersweet occasion. "I'll bring a carriage for you," he had assured her. It was quite a distance up to the von Shuck dwelling for an old woman to walk.

When they arrived at the chalet next morning, the site was ready—tombstone already erected—and the man from the mortuary on hand. The mortician spoke a few words over Herr von Shuck, and then made his way back down Feldberg. The gravediggers finished the deed. Frau Puck had been a very pleasant, supportive companion and that made the morning easier. Hamlet helped her back into the carriage and started to get in himself when the woman glanced toward a low rock building behind the chalet.

"Now I remember! There is a chest in the barn, down there."

"A chest?" Hamlet asked, hardly able to believe his ears.

"Yes. It belongs to Herr von Shuck. I forgot about it until I saw the barn."

"You don't say!" Hamlet said with interest.

"A long time ago, a letter came from ship yard. My husband, Jakob, God rest his soul, was your father's friend and Herr von Shuck was gone; so, he opened it. It says to pick up his trunk. Jakob brought it home and took it back up the mountain. I think he put it in your father's rock barn over there."

Katrina, who had been on hand all morning, couldn't wait for that adventure! She started to make a mad dash down the slope, but on second thought, food, at that very moment, sounded better. She remembered all too well the old world German cooking and she was not about to miss it.

"I'll look in the barn this afternoon," Hamlet said, even though his heart was already racing toward it. Frau Puck had invited Hamlet to lunch and the noon hour was near. He wouldn't want to spoil her plans for the meal. So, down the mountain they went to her cottage where she already had the table set. Hamlet sat in her drawing room smoking his pipe while his hostess filled the house with all sorts of tantalizing aromas from the kitchen. He really was hungry and this was sure to be real German fare. Soon Frau Puck came for him. "Okay. We eat now."

Such food Hamlet had never tasted. There was roulade beef, spatzle noodles, hot sauerkraut, warm brown bread, German beer to drink and Black Forest cake oozing with cherries for dessert.

Even Katrina, unbeknownst to the humans, ate her fill. It had been a long time since she had had a good German meal! Nixes, of course, do not depend on human foodstuffs for nourishment, but most find it a pleasant experience.

After they were finished eating and had exchanged small talk, Hamlet excused himself to go back up the mountain to his father's place. Normally, he would have enjoyed a nap after such a repast; but the chance that his father's sea chest could be in the barn made him forget all about sleeping.

Katrina had tucked herself into the brim of his hat for an easy ride back up to the barn. She thought of the last time she had ridden on that hat and the adventure in Indianapolis at the Red Key where she had found Friedrich.

THE FORGOTTEN CHEST

Ivy covered the rock structure so profusely that one could hardly tell that the mound beneath it was a barn. After a bit of clearing the heavy growth away, Hamlet found the door with its rusty iron hinges. The latch was rusted shut and he could not budge it. The thick wood door felt like it had a coat of resin on it and had withstood many years of weather. Looking around for something to force it open, he spied a round, black rock to use for a mallet. He pounded the latch once, twice, three times before it broke loose and set the door ajar. Cobwebs shrouded the doorway and fell down on Hamlet and Katrina as they edged the door open. The dust the webs held made Hamlet sneeze repeatedly. It was dark inside because vines covered the one window opening. He stepped back out the door, walked around to the side to cut them away with his pocketknife to let some light in, and went back inside. The light from the window fell directly into the middle of the room and, there, to Hamlet's great joy, sat an old black dust covered, dome-lidded sea chest with a large, heavy padlock on the front. In a moment, he found it locked tight. Hamlet shivered in the damp of the half underground rock barn trying to decide what to do next. "I could try breaking it with the same rock I broke in with," he pondered; "or I could try to get the chest outside and up to the house to find something to pry it open." He decided on the latter.

The chest was heavy, to be sure; but he managed to drag it out into the light and up a grassy incline to the dooryard of the chalet. "Now," he said to himself out loud, "to find some way to get it open. Might as well try going inside to see what I can find."

It wasn't too difficult. The door was unlocked, and unlike the barn door, he opened it with ease. Years of dirt and dust had settled on everything that met the eye, but the interior looked like somebody had just stepped out for the evening and never came back. It was fully furnished and in what seemed to be good repair. It was a serendipitous moment for the old weaver. "So this is it?" he marveled. "Underneath all this sediment is my childhood."

For a while, Hamlet forgot about the chest outside and began to explore the spacious home of his past. Lofts on both the east and west walls of the chalet flanked the living area. A rafter-high, fireplace-chimney edifice split the loft into two sections. Four ladders led up to them and stood in place where Johann had left them. Lofts had always fascinated Hamlet and he explored all four with awestruck eyes before exploring the rest of the house.

There was a kitchen built around the marvelous stone fireplace to the east and doors leading into what appeared to be side rooms. The first door Hamlet tried led to a bedroom with a four-poster bed, a chest of drawers, and a dresser to match. "This must have been Mother and Father's room." For a moment, he thought he felt their presence, but he knew they could not be there—that was so long ago.

Stepping back out, he opened the door to the left of the hearth. Something of an old memory stirred in him—it was the nursery and it had two baby beds. A familiar-looking window looked out onto a neighboring mountain. He knew he had looked out that window many times before from his crib. Some words written on the ends of the beds lay half-hidden in the dust. He took his red muslin handkerchief and scattered the dust until he could see what they were: *Clovis* etched into one and *Claire* into the other. Tears gushed into his old eyes as he realized that these were the same names in the silver pendants, which belonged to him and his departed sister, Sparrow.

He knew beyond a doubt that he really was home.

The whole afternoon had been one of major discovery—first the trunk and then the names on the beds. He was anxious to open the sea chest, but a great weariness began to swim through Hamlet. He realized that he had not stopped to rest since he came back up the hill after lunch. There was a rocking chair beside the cold, lonely fireplace and he brushed it off and sat down, intending to stay only a few moments. It would be dark before he awakened.

Katrina curled up like a kitten in the old purple hat, which rested in his lap. It surely was an adventure hat—an Aladdin's carpet just perfect for a nix to ride.

CHAPTER 21

UNFINISHED DREAMS

An owl had flown down the chimney, now missing its damper, which had long ago rusted and fallen onto the grate. Watcher, that old American Spirit, had arrived sometime while the nix and her charge slept. It was a good time for him to acquaint himself with the charming old chalet that had been Grandfather Hamlet's childhood home. He had spied the unopened sea chest just outside the front door and felt that the relic was of more than a little importance to the wandering man.

His first trip abroad, Watcher was amazed at the ancient and foreign ambiance of his surroundings. "As old as I am in America, I feel young in this place," he told himself. "No wonder the fairies and the European immigrants on Sugar Creek have old souls—it's in their very genes."

Too intrigued to rest after his long journey, Watcher flew up to one side of the loft over the kitchen through which the chimney ran and walked quietly about. He inspected, first, the quality of the beautiful pieces of wood—cherry, walnut, birch—which were stacked in neat piles and then the woodworker's carefully arranged tools, which lay in carpenter trays on the workbench. The face of a half-finished violin looked up at him through the wood shavings as if to say, "I'm waiting…I've been waiting for a very long time…." It was as though Herr von Shuck just got up from his stool and climbed down the ladder and walked out of the house.

The loft on the other side of the beautifully-styled rock chimney held chest after chest of household goods—old linens, stores of long-ago rotted and dried up walnuts and fruit, and spools of yarn that seemed to be waiting for Frau von Shuck to choose from. Standing in the center of the loft was a heavy loom, the size of which Watcher couldn't believe. He wondered how anyone could have carried the entire structure up there in the first place. He decided in the end that the carpenter built the loom piece-by-piece right where it sat. All the room lacked was Frau Gertrude sitting before it, shuttle and yarn in hand.

The owl cast a glance down into the living area below where he noticed, for the first time, a draped object about the size and shape of a spinning wheel. A quick flight down and his strong beak made short work of uncovering it. This was no ordinary spinning wheel. The master wood-carver had tooled the most wonderful mountain scenes, embellished with fields of realistic edelweiss in bloom from any angle. "Herr Johann made this; I'm sure of it!"

Engraved on the sewing box next to it was the likeness of a woman holding two children—one in either arm. "Frau Gertrude and the twins," Watcher marveled, "right down to the very last crease in her smile." She looked like Sparrow.

Below, Hamlet was stirring. Time to get to this business....

MESSENGER FROM AMERICA

Cold to the bone, Hamlet felt a bit disoriented. In the darkness, it took him a moment to remember where he was. A moonbeam reached through the open door to provide the only light in the lonesome room.

Lonesome. That was a strange sensation to Hamlet and he did not like it. He had never felt so alone in his fairy-tale life—not even when he had left the St. Augustine mission on his boyhood quest to find his family.

In only a moment, he remembered the livery horse outside. He'd said he would have it back by dark. Katrina tumbled to the floor when Hamlet's shivering hand grabbed up his hat and plopped it on this head. She had to roll out of the way to escape the heel of his boot when he stood. "Whew!" she gasped landing on her belly, wings erect above her, straining to fly. "Oh, dear!" she fussed as she tried to keep her balance to stand up. "Sometimes these wings are more hindrance than help."

She felt something enfolding her like a shawl and she nearly panicked. "Hold on, Katrina," a familiar voice said. "It's only me."

"Watcher! What are you doing here? You scared me to death!"

"Settle down, now. Everything is okay. I was only trying to help get your wings under control," the owl said, softly laughing. "You are in a state my little nix."

"But..." Katrina was trying to collect her senses.

"No time for buts now," Watcher said, taking Katrina's hand in one foot. "Come on. Grandfather Hamlet is leaving."

The two enchanted friends flew out past Hamlet as he closed the door behind him. Settling on a bower of overgrown wild blackberries, they watched as he dragged his father's heavy trunk over to the carriage. The hungry, disgruntled horse whinnied and pranced a bit while the extra weight increased the burden harnessed behind him. Hamlet took a moment to stroke its mane before climbing onto the seat. Releasing the brake, the weary old gentleman picked up the reins and guided the beast down the mountain while the owl and the nix watched them go.

"So, Katrina," the owl said, still keeping his perch on the blackberry briar. "How are things here on Feldberg? I must say the air currents over the mountain peaks on my way in were hard to navigate. I thought the Appalachians were high, but these mountains make them look like so many hills."

"The Schwarzwald range is high," the nix agreed, "and the Feldberg is queen—the grandest of nature's castles. She reaches right into heaven, I do believe. But tell me, why are you here instead of back at the Enchanted Tree? Is there some emergency? I can't believe you're here."

"Right, Katrina. I bring news from the West. Things are not so good around the mill. Gloom has settled on the Shuck family since young Jon came back without Hamlet. They fear that Grandfather will never return since he found his ancestral home. Jon is despondent since he failed to bring his grandfather back into the family fold and Samuel misses his father. Abigail and Jesse do what they can to try to cheer them, but the mood is catching and even John Clay is hard for Friedrich to deal with. The child pays absolutely no attention to him. I'm afraid your newfound nix will give up in disgust and go back to the Red Key where you found him."

"That is bad news, Watcher. My, oh, my, I don't know what to do. Everything is a mess. I know Hamlet will be lonesome here; I can already feel it. But, he may have his mind made up to stay now that his quest is over."

"Exactly," said the owl. "I was afraid of that. Actually, that is why I came. I never could stand to see good souls in pain like the Shucks of America are suffering now. Alas, things are even worse than I thought. If what you say is true, Hamlet is in pain, too—even if that pain is but loneliness."

Katrina and Watcher grew quiet for a few moments, their minds heavy with despair. Presently, Katrina spoke. "Surely something can be done. Let us see what tomorrow brings. I am going back down to the inn to see what Grandfather Hamlet is doing. I'll see you in the morning."

The owl flew up to the chimney and back down its opening to rest on the mantle for the remainder of the night. He was tired from his trans-Atlantic flight.

Katrina found Hamlet on his deeply piled feather bed, just pulling a quilt up under his chin. His head had hardly touched the down pillow before the sound of low snoring filled the quiet, warm room. The sea chest sat in the middle of the tiny sleeping room just where Hamlet had let it down after pulling it up a short flight of wooden stairs. "Hmm. He still has not opened it. Oh well. I suppose he will first thing tomorrow."

A Visitor at the Chalet

The chest remained padlocked up in his bedroom while Hamlet ate breakfast. Having missed dinner the night before, he was famished. Instead of returning to his room, he went back to the livery again to retain a horse and cart for the day. When he came to the widow's house, he saw Frau Puck shaking a rag rug on her front stoop. She gave him a friendly wave as he drove on past and went on up the mountain.

"Back up the hill, indeed!" the tired horse whinnied. He moved with marked reticence after his ordeal just the day before.

"I don't blame you for your lack of enthusiasm, boy," Hamlet apologized, "Sorry I left you hitched to the carriage all afternoon and evening yesterday while I slept. Do not worry. I'll leave you un-tethered today in the shade."

A stand of wild oats had choked out some of the less desirable undergrowth in the walled-in cemetery. Hamlet removed the harness, turned the horse in it to enjoy the repast, and then closed the iron gate to keep it safe. The livery horse gave a slight playful leap at the unexpected freedom to move about and immediately made his way to the glistening oat morsels. Satisfied, Hamlet reentered the house through the front door to explore its contents a little more closely than he had the day before.

The first thing he saw was the spinning wheel, which Watcher had uncovered the previous evening. "Funny. I didn't see that sitting there yesterday. Ah! It looks like the drape fell off it somehow." The wood was warm and smooth under his touch and he could almost feel his mother's hands flying at her work. She looked at him, up from her likeness on the old sewing box, and knew peace. Now, she had found both her children: first, Claire on the forest floor in America, and, now, Clovis in the arms of their Feldberg Mountain home. Hamlet admired the beautiful chest beside the spinning wheel and knew that, of course, this was the image of his mother with him and his sister.

A quick look around in the light of day led Hamlet back up the four sets of loft stairs and into every corner of the chalet. "I must put this place in order. No reason to pay the innkeeper in town when I have a home here."

"Oh, no," Watcher told Katrina. "He's going to stay. He's gonna clean the place up!"

"Our worst fears have come to pass. Whatever shall we do about the family in America? I was hoping," the nix said, "that we'd return to Indiana. The American Spirits are much more to my liking than the arcane nixes I found here."

"Well," the owl said. "All I know is that this will never do. Let's not panic—the day isn't over yet."

WATER FROM ANOTHER TIME

Hamlet primed the pump outside with water from a crystal brook that trickled into a rock cistern in the edge of the back yard. "Amazing," he said aloud to himself. "It still works after forty years."

"Not so strange," a voice said behind him. "I use it every time I come up the mountain. It's the best water I ever tasted—worth the trip up just to get a jug of water to take back home."

A young man held his hand out as Hamlet turned around. "Hello, Mr. Shuck. I am Frau Puck's grandson, Sir. I am Wolf, Wolf Puck. I hope you don't mind; but I have, for many years, been using your father's water—both for me and my grandmother to drink."

"Not at all," Hamlet said with a puzzled yet pleasant look.

"Sir," Wolf said again. "I just can't imagine meeting a member of the von Shuck royal family. I thought—we all thought—that the line had ended here on Feldberg."

"Royal?" Hamlet asked. "I'm afraid I don't know what you mean."

"I don't understand, Sir," the boy answered.

"Then, that makes two of us. What do you mean royal family?"

Wolf looked at Hamlet in amazement. "You really don't know, do you? Let me see, how can I explain?"

"You call yourself Hamlet Shuck. Your father called himself Johann von Shuck. So do you know what the "von" means?"

"I suppose it's some sort of German term but haven't given it any real thought."

"Well," Wolf said with a little hesitancy in his voice. "It means that your ancestors were of royal birth—you are descended from royalty, Sir."

Hamlet tried to take in the significance of the words the boy had spoken. After a few moments, he said, "Please forgive me. If you only knew the confusion I am feeling…"

The two stood in an awkward silence for what seemed an uncomfortable eon when Wolf had the presence of mind to get beyond the lull in the conversation. "Herr Shuck. My grandmother told me you were up here today and wondered whether you'd found the old trunk in the barn."

Hamlet snapped back to reality. "Your grandmother has been very kind to me; and, yes, tell her I did find my father's sea chest in the old barn."

"Good! She'll be glad to hear it."

"I cannot help but notice, Wolf, that you and your grandmother both speak very good English; in fact, yours is remarkably well spoken.

"Thank you Herr Shuck. My mother was born in London. She and my father met in Heidelberg at University when they were students."

"That would explain it," Hamlet laughed. "Do they live in Feldberg?"

"No. Both are deceased. They died when I was twelve. Grandmother Puck did not have a whole lot, but she took me in until I was old enough to get a job at the toyshop and live on my own.

"I taught her to speak English while I lived there."

"I see," Hamlet said, and thought, "I like this boy."

Wolf stood back to take in the old house, which this regal stranger to the mountain had reclaimed. "So, what are you going to do with it?"

"Needs a lot of work. Thought I would wash the inside down and make it livable while I take a stab at fixing up the place. It's the house I was born in, you know."

"Yes. So I understand," Wolf said. "So, do you need some help? I would be glad to lend a hand. I spend my Saturday's hiking around Feldberg anyway. Might as well put this day off to good use."

"Only," Hamlet said, "if you agree to let me pay you. It will be hard, dirty work, but for two resourceful orphans, such as us, it should not take long. I'd like to move my things up from the inn tomorrow."

"No need for pay," Wolf shrugged, "but, if you insist...."

"I do."

"Let's get started then, Herr Shuck."

"Call me Hamlet. I brought up wooden wash buckets and some brooms in the cart. I'll get them."

"For goodness sake," Katrina cried. "That's just all we need—encouragement to stay on the mountain."

It took all day, but the man and lad swept up the floors, washed down the walls, and cleaned out the cobwebs. By nightfall, a fire was burning on the hearthstone when Wolf took his leave, his pocket several francs heavier. Hamlet had shared cheese and bread with the industrious boy for a simple meal after the day's work. He sat, now, in the chair before the heat and felt pleased that together they had made the rooms fit to inhabit.

"Getting dark," he thought aloud. "Better get the rig back to the stable."

Laying the ashes by, he once again closed the door to the chalet and descended the mountain.

"He's talking to himself," Katrina commented, as the two sprites stood on the front stoop, watching him go. "That's a sure sign he's feeling the sting of loneliness. Maybe he'll want to go home before long."

"I wish you were right," Watcher cooed. "Don't get your hopes up, though. He seems pretty set on moving in tomorrow."

"I know," Katrina said getting up to follow the dear old man. "I'd better go, in case he decides to open the trunk tonight."

"I'll bet," Watcher called after her, "that he waits 'til he moves in here to open it!"

For the third day in a row, Grandfather Hamlet checked out the same horse and cart from the livery—this time signing a bill of sale for them. He had also, in fact, settled his account with the innkeeper and loaded the still unopened chest into the carriage for the trip up. He was getting to know the mountain-side by heart.

It was a beautiful Sunday morning and Hamlet heard the church bells peal below, echoing through the valley and up the walls of Feldberg. He rather wished his family back in America could be there to help celebrate the beauty of his surroundings—the scent of the edelweiss, the pure mountain bell music, and his father's house coming back to life.

After again fastening the horse in the cemetery, he dragged the trunk down off the cart and into the house. "I'll just get a hammer from the loft to open this," he said aloud.

"Talking to himself, again," Watcher noted as he sat hidden from view in the opposite loft. The nix faded to invisibility as she drummed her fingers on the finally-to-be-opened treasure.

"Hello! Herr Hamlet! Are you in here?" Wolf called from the door.

Halfway up the ladder, Hamlet stopped and came back down to greet the boy.

"Thought you'd be in church this morning, son."

"Me, too; but, I couldn't resist what promises to be a perfect day on the mountain. Would you like to take a hike with me all the way to the top?"

"Thanks, Wolf; but the only hike I plan to make today is up the side of the house to make some repairs to the windows and the roof."

"Not even going to take a Sunday off then?" the boy asked.

"Guess not. You must know how anxious I am to get a decent coat of paint on the outside."

"Oh, yes. I think I do know. If I had a place like this, I'd be doing the same thing."

"Work hard, my friend, and someday you will."

"Are you kidding? Times are hard all across southwest Germany. The way things are going, I'll never get out of the closet I sleep in behind the toy shop where I work."

"That bad, huh?" Hamlet commiserated. "I have lived in such a place myself in a mission in St. Augustine, Florida. What do you do at the toy shop?"

"Why," Wolf said, looking up a bit surprised at the question. "I make toys— the marionettes to be exact! Don't think I'll ever get rich doing that, though, will I?"

Hamlet regarded his energetic employee from the day before. "One must be artistic to perform such a craft."

"Well, yes. I am rather good at wood face sculpting. At the shop, I am commissioned by the well to do to make custom dolls that capture likenesses of their children."

"I'd love to see one of your dolls sometime. If you always work as hard as you did for me yesterday, you may go very far, indeed. In the meantime, there's more work here if you're looking to make extra money."

"Really?" the boy could hardly believe his luck. "There is no such thing as "extra" money, Sir. I need every penny I can earn. I am saving up to get enough ahead to ask my sweetheart to marry me. She works down at the shop, too."

"Well. It sounds like you are on a mission. You must work for me to restore this chalet to its former beauty. I will need all the help I can get for the next little while."

"It's a deal, Sir. It will be my great pleasure. I'll work every spare moment I have to help you refurbish the von Shuck family home."

The weeds were whacked, the lawn sewed in rye to choke out the abundant weeds, and the house and trim repaired and painted to its original gingerbread glory. Inside, the newly waxed furniture held a high shine and the barrels and buckets, bins and butter churn cleansed to make ready for life anew at the estate of the Family von Shuck.

The owl and the nix watched in despair as the home came alive again. All the while, the sea chest sat unopened. The situation was getting serious. Hamlet hardly had time to be lonely, as the two had hoped.

An evening came when they heard Hamlet say, "Thank you, Wolf. I believe our task is completed. Thank you very much for your help. I hope the money you have earned will help you toward your plans for marriage."

"Thank you, Herr Shuck. In a way, I'm sorry to see it finished. I have enjoyed every day that I have worked beside you here up Feldberg. By the way, you mentioned a while ago that you would like to see one of my marionettes. I brought one in my haversack today—the image of my grandmother."

Upon inspection, the doll looked the very image of Frau Puck. Hamlet, an artist himself, recognized the rare talent of a true artist. "I must have," he thought to himself, "one of these remarkable dolls. The boy is, already, a master carver."

"Wonderful!" Hamlet acclaimed. "The likeness is your grandmother to the last detail. I don't suppose you'd sell this marionette?"

"I'm sorry, no. This is my best work—an image that I hope lives long after she is gone—God forbid.

"It's late, Herr Shuck—I mean Hamlet," Wolf corrected himself as he stuffed the doll back into its carrier. "I'll say good night then."

"Good night," Hamlet said reluctantly. "Again, thank you for everything. Don't be a stranger and come for water anytime you want."

Hamlet watched the boy until he was out of sight down the well-worn road to town below. The darkness swallowed up the road and boy alike before the German-American grandfather stepped into his beautiful chalet. Across the room, flames licked the bottom of his water kettle, reminding him that a cup of tea was just what he needed before retiring to the comfort of bed in the room, which once had belonged to his father and mother and, then, to his father alone.

When he awakened next morning, the house seemed as empty as a vault— the boy would not be coming to keep him company on weekends and each afternoon after his workday at the toyshop. What Hamlet didn't know was that Wolf had saved enough of his generous wages to rent a small house to fix up for himself and his soon-to-be bride. He had taken a special interest in young Wolf; perhaps, it was because he reminded him of his own grandson, Jon. While traveling with Jon, Hamlet had come to enjoy the young man's energy and enthusiasm for the challenge. "I suppose Jon has been back home for a couple of weeks now," Hamlet thought in passing. "Tonight, I'll write a letter to let them all know I'm fine."

The chalet was stark with emptiness that morning. "I just need a little fresh air," Hamlet said to the walls as he drank leftover tea and broke off a crust of the rich, dark loaf of rye bread that Frau Puck had sent to him with Wolf. He got up and went out, coffee cup in hand.

"I must get some goats," he said aloud to himself, again, "to keep this lawn grazed; and, for sure, a milk cow—and chickens for eggs. I will need a garden. I wonder when the best time is to plant a garden in this climate. I'll ask Frau Puck. She'll be sure to know."

The day was getting hot by the time Grandfather Shuck had walked the perimeter of the two acres, and the time of noon was at hand. He walked up to the house and wondered what was in his larder to prepare for lunch. Cheese again. He ate it and sat in his rocker waiting…waiting for something, anything to happen.

A fitful nap and Hamlet sat up with a start. "The sea chest. I could open the sea chest!

"No," he reconsidered. "It is not mine alone to reclaim." Sitting back in his rocker, Hamlet felt an overwhelming loneliness. "I'm homesick," he told the hearth broom before him and dropped his face into his hands.

WOLF PUCK

Two weeks of Saturdays came and went and Wolf did not come to visit Hamlet. Each time the weekend came Grandfather Shuck watched for the lad to come hiking up the road. The hours inched by while he watched and hoped the widow Puck's grandson would come for some fresh water. Monday morning came and Hamlet was bound for the village, in particular, to stop by the grand-mother's house on the way…

"…just to say hello," he called to her over the low fence around her dwelling.

"It is good to see you, Herr Shuck. How are you getting along up on your mountain?"

"Very well, thank you," he lied. "And how is Wolf? I haven't seen him for a while."

"Busy. You know he is to be married on Saturday next. He fixes up a little hut for his Fraulein and everything. Very busy."

"Actually, no, I didn't know that the marriage was that soon! So, he has found a cottage to fix up?"

"He says you pay him well—better than the place where he makes the marionettes. He is very happy nowadays."

"It was worth every franc. He is a hard worker and I wish him much happiness.

"So, the wedding is next Saturday?"

"Uh-huh, at the church over there at ten-thirty," she pointed as she spoke.

The church was a small parish church where the Puck family had been members for generations. Wolf's mother had taught English to several of the locals in the community of the church before her demise. His father had served the church as sexton. The Puck pew was on the right-hand side of the sanctuary. Little did Hamlet know the von Shuck pew was just two rows in front of it.

"Won't you come to his wedding? Wolfgang would be very proud to have you."

"Are you sure?"

"Of course. I tell him you are coming. We eat here afterward. You come, too?"

"I'll plan on it. Good-bye, then! Have a nice day, Frau Puck."

Hamlet did not attend the wedding. He left, instead, a money envelope with Frau Puck to give to Wolf after the wedding. The day found him alone on his mountain grooming the old cemetery as yellow fall leaves tumbled and swirled about him. There was much work to do before winter.

CHAPTER 22

DOCTOR MACK'S NEMESIS

Hamlet's entire world now revolved around Feldberg Mountain, or so it seemed. Nevertheless, sometimes, when he saw an especially beautiful crop of wildflowers, he thought about his old friend Shane's 47-acre wood and knew that even the majestic Edelweiss could not compare with its Daddy's Breeches. Once, during a visit to town, he happened to see a child hanging onto its mother's skirt tail and remembered the morning he had spent drinking coffee in Abigail's warm kitchen, playing with John Clay. Another time, he visited a pub in the village where a riot of German caricatures, which were painted on one wall, reminded him of the old gang at the Red Key. "Ah," he sighed, "but that was an ocean away." The truth was that he often thought about his family and friends, wondered what they were doing, and hoped they were in good health.

Indeed, back in America, the Indiana fall found a community of farmers bringing in the harvest. Autumn also brought poison to the Indiana air—and with it, illness. Doctor Mack Riley often wondered what it was about the beautiful, wooded land on Sugar Creek that turned it into a deadly wilderness. On one particular evening, something happened that began to put this ongoing question into a feasible hypothesis.

Darkness had fallen when Doctor Mack closed the door to his office for the night. He crossed the street to the livery stable where soft light was emanating from the wide barn doors.

It was late. Mack Riley often worked long into the evening to do battle with his worst enemy—the equinoctial storms of disease. He felt personally responsible when ague and milk fever, the strange illness that killed many people, called on the heels of both summer and winter. He was the doctor, why couldn't he cure his patients? The very lives of his friends, family and patients were in his hands—and God's. He had searched hard to discover why these seasonal maladies laid so many in the grave.

Mack was usually the stable's last patron of the day. Mistletoe, the son of his father-in-law's old roan, El Navidad, was already outside, hitched to the same old cherry buggy that El Navidad had pulled. Keren-happuck had driven it one Christmas Eve before they were married to visit him at his father's mill. The carriage, though dingy and dark from years of weather, was what he used almost exclusively now to make doctor calls. A dingy green sign over the stable door swayed on its rusty iron hanger, creaking in the gentle breeze. Barely able to make out its faded red lettering, Mack knew by heart that the shingle read, "Elisha Adams, Livery Stable, since 1819."

The doctor had known Elisha since his father first brought the family up the Ancient Trail from Kentucky. Elisha helped his father find a suitable place on Sugar Creek to build a mill. A lively village emerged around the mill and John Riley became the first county sheriff. John soon moved to Franklin and Elisha opened a livery stable in Edinburgh, a small village just south of the mill; yet the two remained friends until Sheriff John passed in 1854.

The white-haired stable owner walked out, leaning heavily on his hickory cane, and latched the double doors for the night. Mack smiled and said, "Cool evening, Elisha."

"Yes it is, Doctor Mack," the livery master returned and started away. After a few steps, he turned around abruptly. "Dang me! I almost forgot! Jessie Shuck sent Jon down to ask you to stop by their place on your way out to the old cabin tonight…said she thinks the youngun broke his arm playing slips in the dark last night…said it was all swollen up like a watermelon today. You were busy, so I told him I'd tell you when you came for your rig."

"Thank you, Elisha. I had better hurry if I am to make another stop. The wife's expecting, you know. I worry about her when I'm late getting home these days. We're staying at the old cabin to be near to her parents; she's real close."

"Now, don't you worry," Elisha said. "Miz Rose and Shane are there. They'll look after her."

"Well, yes. I am glad for that."

Elisha shuffled off to the swing on his front porch. He lived next door to the stable. It was his habit to wait there for the supper bell—a bell that would not ring until the doctor was well out of sight. It wouldn't do for Doctor Mack to know that Elisha's wife, Ruth, waited supper every night until he closed his medical office and picked up his horse and trap. Elisha watched from his seat in the swing while the doctor methodically placed his medical bag in its usual spot on the buggy floor, hoisted himself onto the seat and lit the coach lantern. Taking up the reins, Mack coaxed Mistletoe to go.

"Dark already," Mack grumbled. "It has to be Jon Clay; the baby is too little to play a game like slips. It seems that that boy is always breaking something or sick from something. Oh well, I just wish I could have gotten away earlier!"

The roan pulled the buggy north out of town. Mistletoe knew the way out to the farm from repetition. Riding along in the moon light, Mack sat back in the seat, barely holding the reins. His thoughts were upon Keren-happuck. "It can't be long now…Hope she's okay…" He could feel the barometer falling.

The birth of their first child imminent, Mack also thought about all the other children he had delivered and doctored. He'd seen both happy times, when they would come into the world, and sad times, when he could not cure them from pneumonia or small pox or any number of ailments for which he had no antidote.

Dr. Riley was a tenacious physician—hungry for better remedies and procedures for his patients. His training had come from watching other doctors, reading medical journals and just plain on-the-job trial and error. There just didn't seem to be any successful treatment for some illnesses.

His patients seemed to be healthier in the wintertime. It was the only time he could tuck rest into his schedule. However, in early spring, when the first white wildflowers began to bloom in the moist, black ground in the wooded terrain, mixed feelings of hope and dismay stirred in his heart. He tried to keep positive, but before summer even arrived, he would find his days consumed with another season of suffering and death.

He asked himself repeatedly, "Why do so many die here?" There was plenty of nourishing food to eat and trees to build sturdy, warm homes. He'd read that the childhood death rate was much lower in other settled regions of America. "What is it about Indiana?" Now that he would have a child of his own, Mack had an even more desperate desire to find the answer.

Over his first years of practice, he had noticed patterns from certain ailments; but he had not been able to put his finger on what caused them. The only thing he knew for sure was that the sickness would come and he would be busy. He was so busy, in fact, that on weekends he drove Keren down to stay in the summer cabin so that she could put out a garden there with Rose and Shane. The long days and nights of a doctor's wife sometimes became monotonous for Keren and she enjoyed going back to the farm to visit. It was always a welcome change of pace and Keren became, perhaps, closer to her mother than she ever had been before. Together they made huge gardens in the black loam at the edge of the tree line where they planted in the spring and reaped in the fall.

This year was no different, except that, since Keren was expecting, they had temporarily closed their house in Edinburgh and moved to the little cabin on Sugar Creek in midsummer. Keren needed to be with her family now, since her husband was gone all hours of the day and night.

Oh, yes. Mack was, indeed, care-laden upon this evening. With half-closed eyes, he rode along in the dust of the five-mile dirt road to the Shucks and home. The night swallowed him when clumps of roadside trees occasionally came between the orange harvest moon and the carriage, but his mind was fertile in the quiet countryside. A chill gradually gripped him on one particularly long stretch of darkness as he felt a premonition that before this night was over his life would change. It wasn't about the baby. Oh, yes, he knew the power of the full moon and a falling barometer and thought the baby would come; but, from the back of his mind, something else flashed forward like chalk on a blackboard—the word **FEVER**.

Mosquitoes

Mack drove through the open gate that led back the Shuck's lane. He was tired and hungry and felt an anxious chill run over him. "Why tonight?" he muttered, "That kid." Mistletoe pulled the rig up the lane to a stop at the dooryard.

Jesse was first out the door. She had seen his lantern swinging in the night.

"You poor pretty thing," she said to Mistletoe, rubbing his nose. "You just go and go, don't you boy? Hi, Mack!"

"Good evening, Jesse." He, too, patted his animal. "He's a good horse, never been sick a day in his life. I wish I could say that for my patients!"

Jessie laughed. "Well, come on in, Mack. Thanks for coming. I got a boy that's hurtin' a right smart tonight."

"What happened?" Mack asked, stepping through the door.

Jon was sitting at the kitchen table with a cup of coffee. Before Jessie could say anything, he answered Mack's question, "Oh! He busted his arm acting a fool in the wet grass last night."

Jessie poured Mack a cup of coffee. "Want some pie?"

"No. It will ruin my supper. I imagine the women are keeping it warm for me."

"Keren's due soon, isn't she?" Jessie asked.

"Any moment," Mack said, hoping to get through the small talk and on to the boy so he could get home. "Well, where's the patient?"

Jon got up and took Mack to the loft where the children slept. The boy was lying on a straw tick. In the background, Mack heard the low rumble of thunder and saw a flash of lightning. Downstairs, Jesse was calling up to him, "I told that child to come on in from the dampness, he'd catch his death, or that the mosquitoes would eat him alive! I never dreamed he'd break his arm coming in!"

Mack was examining John Clay by then, but when he heard Jesse's words—the same, repetitive admonitions he had heard so often from other mothers as they prattled at their children to come in for the evening—his heart jumped, and he looked up at Jon and said, "Mosquitoes!"

"What?" Jon asked with a puzzled look.

Mack tried to think for a moment about what he was going to say, but he shopped short. "If I get into this, I'll never get home…better get this arm set and get out of here…

"Oh! Hum, yes. There are a lot of mosquitoes this year."

Mack felt the arm again and punched here and there, while the boy howled and jerked his arm around. "From the swelling, I suspect it's just a fracture. Nothing feels broken," he said. Doctor Mack took some splints out of his bag and asked Jon for some strips of muslin to hold them in place and to make a sling. When he was finished, he said, "Keep him in bed for a few days so he won't be tempted to use that arm."

Patting the boy on the head, he climbed back down to the kitchen. "Give him some of this tonic for pain three or four times a day. It will make him sleepy, so you probably will not have any trouble keeping him down. Go ahead and give him some now."

Jessie took the vial of medicine, opened the cupboard, and took out a spoon. She started up the stairs when she heard Mack say, "Jess. I wouldn't run off so fast, but I need to get home. I believe we'll have that baby tonight."

"You sure you don't want some pie first?"

He did not wait to answer her. His mind on fire, he was out the door and in the carriage, heading for home. "I need to think," he said to himself. "I need to think. It all seems to be making sense…the mosquitoes, the mud, the damp…the fever. They all seem to come together at the same time of the year." The swamps of the wet seasons—spring and fall—were perfect breeding grounds for disease-carrying mosquitoes and rodents. Mack realized that the marshes probably contributed to the high death rate in central Indiana.

It was hard for the kindhearted Doctor Mack to lose any patient; but when a child died, he grieved as piteously as a banshee did.

Note: In real life, Dr. Smiley lost most of his own eleven children to illness even though he fought valiantly for a cure. One unsympathetic person said, "He wasn't much of a doctor because he couldn't even keep his own children alive." Early medicine had light years to go.

CHAPTER 23

LIZZY IS BORN

Mack was late. Supper was ready and everyone was hungry.

"There's no need for the rest of us to eat a cold supper just because Mack is late," Rose said. "I'll keep his plate warm over the fire. Let's the rest of us eat."

Keren-happuck, Shane and Rose sat down at the big cherry table. Rose had fried rabbit and potatoes for the evening meal—a supper that would be much better eaten freshly prepared. Shane gave grace and they ate the rabbit and the rest. After dinner, he rocked before a hearty fire in the fireplace, while his mother's old peacock slept on the floor beside him.

"Mother," Keren said, while helping to clear the table. "The baby hasn't moved much since yesterday. Do you think something's wrong?"

"Child. That is the surest sign that the baby is on its way."

"It is?"

"Uh-huh. It's the baby resting up before the birth. Oh, they're smart little creatures, even before they're born."

"I wish Mack would get home. I feel so tired. The wind has picked up and it feels like rain. I watched the lane for the lantern on the buggy all during supper. Where is he?"

"Now, you know its hard telling. A doctor's life is hard to schedule. Say, you aren't having any pains are you?" Rose asked suspiciously.

"Not really. It's just pressure. See, the bulge of the baby is in the bottom of my belly, not up high like it has been."

"Oh? Let's see." Rose pushed back Keren's apron to see. "Oh, my! There's no mistake about that! I hadn't noticed. Keren, you are about to be a mother!

Shane looked over at his daughter. "Here. Why don't you sit down and rest. I will help your mother with the dishes. Don't worry, Mack will be here soon."

Keren took his rocker and absently let her hand drop to stroke the old peacock. "How are you doing Brother Peacock? Do you miss Grandmother?" She had a slight backache and it did feel good to sit.

In the background, Keren heard her father talking to her mother over the clang of the dishes: "I think that tomorrow we need to re-stuff the scarecrow. The rabbits are starting to eat the turnip leaves." Smiling and drowsy, she felt like a small child again listening to her parents plan to tend the scarecrow. She felt safe and warm and dropped off to sleep feeling all of six years old again.

The lantern on Dr. Mack's carriage flickered in the distance as Rose and Shane rested on the porch—dishes dried and put away and Keren-happuck sleeping soundly before the fire inside. Leaves swirled about the yard in the evening breeze and dampness hung in the air. There was no dew on the grass because Mother Nature had gathered it for the coming rain. "I'm glad he's finally home," Rose sighed. She got up and lifted her skirts to step over the threshold. "I'll just go put his supper out. I hope it's still fit to eat."

Shane sat, pipe in hand, while Mack and Mistletoe made their way up the lane. He would feed and groom the horse; he knew Mack would be tired after such a long day. An Irish immigrant, the soon-to-be grandfather felt how fortunate he was to own, free and clear, the 47-acre wood, which virtually enfolded his family in love and well being from the very day that he and Rose set foot in it.

"Home from the war, medic?" he asked jokingly. "Here. I'll put him up. Your supper is ready. Keren is inside asleep."

Mack was exhausted and hungry and gave no objection to Shane's offer. He walked in the cabin, put his hat and jacket on his usual peg by the door, and washed his hands and face.

Rose's dry sink was the centerpiece of the entry cove just inside the door. Clean hand-embroidered linen towels, as usual, hung neatly over wooden dowels on either side of it; a white china bowl and pitcher with hand-painted pink English roses brought a touch of elegance to their home. Candle sconces, on either side of a matching china mirror over the sink, held bees-wax candles, which she lit each evening before dinner, to welcome Shane or any visitor at day's end.

"Hello, Mom," he greeted Rose, noting that Keren was still sound asleep. "That sure smells good. It's been a long time since I ate."

"Well, you'd better eat up now, for I have a feeling this may be a long night. I think Keren has started her labor."

Mack smiled at the prospect of the baby's long-awaited arrival. "I'm glad I made it back in time. I thought all day that it might be tonight or tomorrow. How's she feeling?"

"Oh, fine, when she went to sleep—just a feeling that the time was near."

"Okay. I'll get her back over to our cabin as soon as I eat."

Rose poured Mack a cup of steaming sassafras tea and turned up the flame on the oil lamp on the dining table. Shane soon came in from the barn with a load of firewood in his arms. The logs in the wood box shifted as he added the new pieces, which bumped against the sides with a thud. Keren stirred and opened her eyes. She saw her father just taking a piece off the top to add to the glowing embers.

"Is Mack home, yet?" she asked, as Shane stoked the fire.

"He is eating his supper. Mack! Your sleepyhead is awake."

Mack had just finished and crossed the room to help his wife up out of the rocking chair. "Come on, Miss Sleepyhead, time to go home."

"Mack," she uttered unsteadily through a pang of discomfort as she started to stand. "I think you'd better carry me. I don't feel so good."

"Do you want us to go with you, Keren?" Rose asked while a brief phantom memory pain shot through her.

"No, Mother. You get some rest. We may need you more later."

"Okay, but, let your father at least help get you to the bed. I'll get your shawl."

Shane agreed. "It's raining. I'll get the carriage and take you both down. I'll just help you get in the house."

"Good idea," Mack said. He took the shawl from Rose and wrapped it around Keren snugly where she sat. "I'll get my coat and hat; be right back."

Shadow fairies danced on the wall behind the sconce candles as Mack carried Keren past them on the way out...

Down in the sycamore, Pitt and Keen danced with excitement and wished against hope that Watcher and Katrina were back home for the happy occasion.

When Rose woke up, daylight was breaking. "Shane! Wake up! It is almost daylight! We've slept the whole night through, and there hasn't been a word from Mack."

Shane stretched and rubbed his eyes. "Don't be so excited—that means she must be doing okay."

"Come on, get up! Let's go see."

"Breakfast first. We can take some down to them after we eat."

"But...we ought to..."

"No, Rosie. Give them a chance to wake up. He would have let us know if the baby was coming. Remember how long it took for Keren-happuck to be born?"

"Oh, okay. Nevertheless, let's hurry. That is precisely why I want to go to Keren. It was a long, awful dance until Stargazer came the day she was born."

"But, Mack's a doctor, Rose," Shane reminded her.

"Doctor, yes; Stargazer, no."

"You sure did put a lot of store in that Indian woman," Shane said and placed a hand on Rose's shoulder.

"If I remember right, you were mighty glad when she got there, yourself," Rose reminded him.

While waiting for breakfast, Shane went out to feed the animals and chickens. The smell of biscuits baking and smoked ham sizzling in an iron skillet followed him. It was a crisp morning in the woods and the first frost of the season glistened on the grass. The aphrodisiac of the cold air in his face, and the aroma of coffee crawling after him all the way to the chicken house, acted like a tonic on Shane; he whirled and kicked his heels like a young boy with not a care in the world. When he got to the barn, he gave each of the horses an extra scoop of oats. "Gettin' cold," he told them. "You'll need this to keep you warm. It's autumn."

Breakfast finally over, Rose and Shane walked down to the old cabin.

Basket in hand, Rose's mouth flew open as she stepped across the threshold. Dr. Mack was sitting before the fire with a bundle in his hands. She shoved the basket handle over Shane's forearm and hurried across the room.

"The baby! It's here!" she gasped.

Mack had a smile on his face and looked contented as he rocked back and forth in the chair.

"Shush! You'll wake Keren."

A quick glance through the bedroom door assured Rose that her daughter was still sleeping soundly. She bent down to pull the blanket back from her new grandchild's face. "Oh, look at you—the image of your mother! Is this a boy or girl?"

"She's a girl; born just before midnight."

"Before midnight?" Rose caught her breath.

"Why didn't you pull the bell for us to come?" Shane asked in surprise.

"No need," Mack laughed. "Keren hadn't been in bed for an hour before she had the first strong labor pain. Five minutes later, she had another one and the baby was born. Two pains. That is all. I couldn't believe it, but there was no mistaking the sound of the baby's first cry. We saw no need of interrupting your sleep. I never saw such an easy birth in any of my patients."

"How is Keren-happuck?" Rose asked, looking now toward the bed where her daughter was sleeping. "Is she doing okay?"

"She's fine, but tired. She didn't go back to sleep until almost daylight; and, this little one, she seems to be as content as a kitten. I can already tell she likes to be rocked. Do you want to hold her?"

"Come here, Little One." Rose took her granddaughter in her arms and sat in Mack's rocker. "I brought breakfast. It is in the basket there. Help yourself."

Shane handed Mack the basket of food. "So, have you given her a name?"

"We have—Elizabeth Rose."

"Elizabeth Rose Riley," Rose said. "Such a beautifully lyrical name."

"We'll call her Lizzy," Mack added. "What do you think, Grandpa? Doesn't she look like a Lizzy?"

Shane smiled and walked over for a closer look at the child. Just at that moment, Elizabeth Rose opened her tiny glittering eyes. "Oh, dear. She has the same mischievous green eyes that her mother had when she was born. And, yes, she looks exactly like a Lizzy!"

"She looks," Rose philosophized as she kissed the baby's cheek, "like our next generation."

Shane chuckled: "I hope the world is ready for her!"

Keren-happuck stirred and sat up in her bed. "Good morning, Grandma and Grandpa!"

"Well, hello there, sleeping beauty. You're a mother!" Shane answered happily.

"So, how do you like her?" Keren asked her mother.

Rose glowed as she got up to take the baby to her mother. "She's perfect."

"Oh, what a happy day!" Keen squealed from the small rock ledge built into one side of the stone fireplace. She and Pitt had noticed the midnight lights burning several hours before and been present for the whole event.

"Look at Rose," Pitt joined in. "I haven't seen her so cheerful since before Keren got married and moved away from home."

"Come on," Keen urged him and stood up. "Let's go make the announcement in the woods! Black Hawk and Chelsea will be waiting to hear. Too bad hawks and ground squirrels aren't allowed in the house."

The two dematerialized and reappeared inside the sycamore. That night, the fairy ring would be gleeful and crowded as the American Spirits celebrated the beginning of a completely new chapter of life on Sugar Creek. And, to boot, Friedrich was still among their number.

CHAPTER 24

A TWIST OF FATE

He was on the evening stage when it came to rest in front of the Riley-Willard Hotel in Franklin. Famished and tired from the dusty road trip, the man signed the burgundy leather guest register with the ornate quill provided for that purpose. The very act of signing one's name in such an eloquent fashion set the stage for the rest of the visitor's stay. A winding staircase, carpeted in fine, formal, plaid Scottish wool, led to the guest rooms on the second floor. A small, cozy lounge in a south alcove enticed both locals and travelers into its warmth. The stranger took a side table just inside the door and settled his long legs beneath it, thankful that the creature comforts of food and beverage were only a kitchen away.

A small kerosene lamp flicked its light across his tired, creased face, while the barmaid took his order. A moment later, he released a huge sigh, and a smile of what seemed like relief slowly spread across his face.

His eyes twinkled orange and yellow reflections from the crackling fire in the brown marble fireplace as he looked around the room. For a moment, he rested the back of his head against the wall and noticed the design in the embossed tin ceiling above him. "What a wonderful place," he thought, and closed his eyes. After gathering his senses, he relaxed and set back upright in his chair. No one in the dining room looked even remotely familiar to the white-haired wayfarer, and the locals speculated on the stranger's provenance.

Hamlet was home.

Germany had changed the old master weaver. Never in his life's journey had he been as lonesome as he was on Feldberg Mountain. His only friend there had been Wolf, and Wolf's recent wedding had interrupted rather permanently their close companionship. The fact of the young man's eagerness to start a family with his new wife had made Hamlet stop to think about his own family back in Indiana. Jon, with Jesse and their little ones now, had been so like Wolf when he started—eager and strong. And Samuel...how he had missed his son's affections and yearned to tell him about his ancestors. "I'm glad to be going home," Hamlet allowed. "My quest is finally over."

On the morrow, the old weaver would post the letter, which he penned to Wolf on his journey home, and then hire a trap to carry his father's chest and a satisfied soul out to his heart's own Sugar Creek and the rest of his life.

The End

EPILOGUE

Dear Wolf,

You were the one who primed our pump for all the years we were away from the mountain—excellent stewardship should be rewarded. For that, I give your wife my mother's loom to clothe your children.

You were the Good Samaritan who welcomed me back home into my father's fold when he could not; and, for that, I give you his tools to make a living. A man of any age rarely performs such a deed.

You upheld the royalty of the von Shuck name by helping me to understand the nuances of the language. Thank you, indeed, for helping me to restore the ancestral chalet to its former glory.

Now, for that, I propose a trade: For four marionettes made with your own hands, I will give unto your good hands the title to our Feldberg home and the land upon which it stands. May it bring you all the joy and wealth its acres offer and your family a place to call home.

And now, to borrow the ending of a fairy tale, may you live happily ever after.

Yours,

Hamlet Shuck

P.S. Please send likenesses from your own imagination of a man and woman and two children—twin boy and girl—to Hamlet Shuck, % Riley's Mill, Johnson County, Indiana, America.

Enclosure: Title for the Johann von Shuck estate, Feldberg Mountain, Germany.

Afterword

Something was going on down in Peter Henry's bottoms below the Ancient Trail ridge. The light from a single lantern was the only sign of it, at least from where Squire Henry, Peter's son, stood on his own back porch. "A hunter," he decided and retired to his bed for the night. He was the sole witness to the deed Hamlet Shuck was about that late autumn night; but Squire never in the whole of his life, knew it…

Hamlet had completed his genealogical quest, which led him to Germany, to his full satisfaction. His family, of course, was overjoyed upon his return to Indiana, even though the weaver went back to his Indianapolis studio to work.

The American Spirits who resided in the grand sycamore on Sugar Creek reunited, now that the nix and the enchanted owl were back from their caregiver duties in Germany. Katrina and Watcher sometimes wondered whatever happened to the sea chest that Hamlet retrieved from his father's barn. The question remained unanswered, as the years flew by, until one day far into the future…

From 1830 to 1850, frontier life flourished as babies were born and diseases doctored. Thousands more brave, hardy settlers crossed the Appalachian Mountains in search of a better life. Many eventually flocked into Texas and California and other western lands, which belonged to Mexico; but the Johnson County Sugar Creek pioneers stayed put; they had found a better life—right there.

Cyrus McCormick, back in Virginia, had patented the reaper in 1834 and the Henry's owned one, as well as others up and down Sugar Creek. After that, the innocence of the land was history.

Just as the nix had predicted, even before the child was born, Lizzy Riley was to become quite locally famous as she grew amidst the patchwork of old souls on Sugar Creek. As a true daughter of renaissance, she was the quintessential heartbeat of the Riley Mill community, as you will see in *The Storyteller Quilt*, Book Three of the *Sugar Creek Anthologies of Jesse Freedom*.

References

Books:

Banta, David D., *History of Johnson County*. Chicago: Brant & Fuller. 1888.

Branigin, Elba, *History of Johnson County, Indiana*. Indianapolis: B.F. Bowen, Inc. 1913.

Time-Life Book editors, *The Mighty Chieftains*, The American Indians Series.

Alexandria, Virginia. Time-Life Books. 1993.

Bergen, John V., Illustrated Historical Atlas, Johnson County, Indiana, 1820-1900. Indianapolis: William B. Burford. 1983-1984. Sponsored by Johnson County Historical Society, Franklin, Indiana

Illustrated Historical Atlas, Johnson County, Indiana, 1820-1900. Indianapolis: William B. Burford. 1982-84. Sponsored by Johnson County Historical Society, Franklin, Indiana.

Newsletters & Journals:

Henry, Rachael, editor. *Nostalgia News,* the Johnson County Historical Museum Newsletter. Franklin, Indiana. (October, 1978) Issue 6, p. 12.

Liggett, Judith, editor. *Smiley Mill 4-H Club Journal,* the Smiley Mill 4-H Club. Franklin, Indiana. 1982 and 1984 4-H Fair editions.

Robbins, Judith, journalist: "The Sugar Creek Anthologies of *Jesse Freedom.*" 1986-1988.

Note: *Jesse Freedom* is a pen name used by Judith Fowler Robbins during her cabin years.

Also by the author…

American Spirits

Judith Fowler Robbins

"The Sugar Creek Anthologies of Jesse Freedom Series"

American Spirits
ISBN: 0-595-22460-1
Book One 2002
"The Sugar Creek Anthologies of Jesse Freedom" series

- **The Indianapolis Star** wrote, "Judith Fowler Robbins of Indianapolis draws on her childhood in Johnson County, Indiana, in "American Spirits." The story is set in the 19th century and grew out of journal entries Robbins kept while living along Sugar Creek. It tells of the American Indians and early white settlers in the area and the animals who lived there with them. The book has a charm and innocence readers will find enchanting."

- **The Journalist** (Franklin College magazine) wrote, "While living in a cabin along Sugar Creek—just down the road from her childhood home—Robbins began interviewing older neighbors in the Smiley's Mill area of Johnson County, just east of the Franklin College campus. During the same time, as a 4-H leader, she encouraged Needham Township 4-H'ers to learn more about the neighborhood in the "People in My World" project. A good read."

- **The Daily Journal** (newspaper) wrote, "It's a book mothers could read to children...A fast read, the book is based on historical fact and would be suitable for upper elementary and teen-age students...adults, especially, get caught up in it, too."

- **Available** from the: **Indiana Historical Society**, Indianapolis, Indiana, and the **Johnson County Museum**, Franklin, Indiana, as well as online from all major booksellers.

About the Author

Judy Robbins grew up on a farm in Indiana. She graduated from Indiana State University and followed a career in journalism. She published her first book, *American Spirits*, in 2002. Judy lives in Indianapolis, where she is at work on the final book in *The Sugar Creek Anthologies* trilogy.

0-595-30084-7

CPSIA information can be obtained at www.ICGtesting.com
Printed in the USA
LVOW11s2217270214

375506LV00001B/198/A